# Midnight Dancer

Mory was close now and vulnerable. Suddenly her courage failed and she rode Dancer towards the main track. Too late! There was a deep bark and the large grey dog leapt from the garden sniffing the air. Mory turned away in a panic. The movement caught the dog's eye and it bounded forward. Snorting, Dancer sprang to escape. The huge, fallen trunk of an oak tree lay straight across their path. Mory gasped when she saw it but there was no stopping now. Out of the corner of her eye she saw the riders on the ridge. Distracted, she miscounted the strides. One, two, and before she knew it Dancer was in the air. Caught out, Mory could do nothing but let herself fall and she hit the ground with a sickening thud — every bit of breath knocked from her.

D0892946

# Midnight Dancer

## Running Free

by Elizabeth Lindsay

illustrated by Linda Boddy

Hippo

*For Harriet*

Scholastic Children's Books
7–9 Pratt Street, London NW1 0AE, UK
A division of Scholastic Publications Ltd
London ~ New York ~ Toronto ~ Sydney ~ Auckland

First published by Scholastic Children's Books, 1995

Copyright © Elizabeth Lindsay, 1995
Illustrations copyright © Linda Boddy, 1995

ISBN 0 590 55853 6

Typeset by TW Typesetting, Midsomer Norton, Avon
Printed by Cox & Wyman Ltd, Reading, Berks.

10 9 8 7 6 5 4 3 2 1

# Contents

# ONE

# *Grey Ghost*

Cantering along, drizzle-drenched in the half light, Mory let Midnight Dancer have her head. It was a straight stretch, Mory knew it well and the pony needed no asking. She galloped, splashing through puddles without a stumble, to the rock crop peaking the ridge.

"Whoa now, whoa." Reluctantly Dancer slowed. "Better get back," said Mory, stroking the pony's hot, wet neck as she came down to a trot. "I didn't say I was coming up here. I said I was cleaning tack."

Suddenly, from out of the gloom a lean, grey shape lurched towards them. Startled, Dancer whipped round. Mory struggled to stay on as Dancer galloped to escape. Hauling herself upright Mory glanced behind to see the grey shape speed after them.

"Hell's bells! What is it?"

A shrill whistle pierced the gloom and the darting grey shape was gone. But Dancer, gripped by terror, wouldn't stop. Mory braced herself against the stirrups and used emergency tactics. Holding one rein firm she pulled and let go with the other. The third pull unbalanced Dancer enough to slow her.

"Whoa girl, it's gone. Whoa now, whoa." Mory's soothing tones helped settle the pony and she turned to retrace their steps. Dancer, reluctant, pranced sideways, shaking flecks of foam from her mouth. "Just a little way," said Mory, urging her forward. "Just a little way. Come on, girl. Come on." Mory was curious to know what had chased them and besides, going back a short distance might reassure Dancer. But there was nothing. Only the fuzzy white blurr of a sheep bobbing through the heather. Mory looked at her watch and frowned.

"Heck! I'm for it!" She turned for home. Trotting off the ridge pony and rider followed the sheep path into the valley to where Black Rock Farm, grey-stoned and slated, nestled in the rain, its beacon-lit windows signalling a welcome and the lateness of the hour.

Riding into the yard metal hit stone. The tell-tale ring brought David hurrying from the pottery.

"What time do you call this?" Mory had hoped to arrive unnoticed, with time to explore excuses.

"Sorry, Dad. I went for a ride."

"We've eaten without you! Look at you, soaking wet! *And* it's nearly dark."

"I know, I'm sorry." Mory led Dancer into her stable. She knew what was coming next.

"What if anything had happened?" She decided

not to say anything about the frightening grey shape that had caused Dancer to bolt. At least not to her parents.

"But it didn't, Dad, did it?" They were still on edge after her narrow escape from the danger of tracking down the local burglar. Mory untacked Dancer and rubbed her down. Such a lot had happened since they had moved here. Dancer had become her pony and country life was unexpectedly wonderful. Mory poured out her joy in long letters to Hannah far away in Waring where they used to live, bewitching her friend, until she too longed for the summer holidays and the gaunt Welsh hills Mory so vividly described.

"You can go out with the others when you've dried off," she said, stroking Dancer's face. The pony nuzzled her hand. "I know, I know. Here you are." Mory rummaged in her pocket and offered some soggy pony nuts. Dancer chewed appreciatively, watching patiently as Mory carried the soaking saddle and bridle to the tack room. A familiar routine. On her return Dancer whickered. Unable to resist, Mory dug out a second handful of Dancer's favourite food.

"Won't be long," she told the pony and hurried across the yard to the house.

In the porch she pulled off her wellies, hung up her hat and then, full of grovelling apology, went into the kitchen. Her mother was sitting at the table amongst a pile of marking.

"I'm really sorry, Mum. I really am. Only I got carried away. It was fantastic riding in the rain. Going against the elements and all that and ..."

"And what?"

"And you said don't be long the meal was ready and I forgot." Mory put on a woebegone face. "But I'm glad you didn't wait. And I'll do all the washing up."

"Yours is in the oven and the washing up is done." That was a relief. "But ..." Mory's heart sank at the but, "... it's a school day and riding into the hills at this time of the evening must not happen again. Do you understand?" Mory nodded. She understood all right. "And in this weather. You must be mad."

Mory fetched her supper from the oven and put it on the table. It was dry and shrivelled but she didn't care, she was hungry. She took a mouthful and her eyes met her mother's which, all of a sudden, twinkled.

"What's funny?" she managed to ask, her mouth bursting.

"I don't know how you can eat it. It looks disgusting."

"No, no," said Mory. "It's delicious." She crunched the dried potato contentedly.

"In future, do you think you can try and do what you're told?" Sheila sighed. "There aren't that many rules in this house, are there?"

"I will, really I will," said Mory. Her apology over, her mind was already pondering the streaking grey

4

shadow. Did she remember a whistle? It could have been the wind whistling in her ears, Dancer had been galloping fast. But after that the grey beast had gone. She paused in her chewing. It must have been a dog. Her mother recognized the preoccupied look and, with a quizzical raised eyebrow, carried on marking.

When she had finished Mory carried her plate to the sink. She wanted to ring Cara but didn't want her mother to overhear, an impossibility as the phone was by the kitchen door. Cara had become more like a sister than a cousin. That's how Mory felt, living so close, being together so often. Mory liked the feeling. It was warm and companionable. They talked horses for hours. It was urgent that Mory tell Cara of the leaping grey ghost on the ridge. Cara would want to know.

"Is it too late to go up to Llangabby?" she asked, knowing what the reply would be.

"Of course it's too late. It's bedtime. Besides, you need to get out of those wet clothes. Go on, upstairs and have a hot bath."

But Mory had to tell someone. She stopped at Josh's room on the landing. The light was still on.

"Josh?"

"What?"

"Can I come in?" She didn't wait for an answer and found him poring over his ugly, grey space creatures, horrible things, all the rage with the boys at school.

"I'm busy." He was applying green paint to a savage-looking warrior.

"Guess what happened?" said Mory, noticing Josh didn't seem in the least bit interested. "I got chased by a grey ghost." A slight exaggeration but it had its effect. Josh put down his paint brush.

"Pull the other one," he said.

"Okay, okay," said Mory. "I just said grey ghost. But we got chased by something and whatever it was frightened us. Well, Dancer anyway. It was spooky coming out of the gloom like it did."

"What was it?"

"Thinking about it, it must have been a dog. It's the only thing it can have been."

"Weird," said Josh. "Whose?"

"I don't know. There's only us and Llangabby Farm. Nothing else for miles. Mab's the only dog round here."

"Not for long," said Josh. Uncle Glyn's border collie was about to have puppies.

A long, loud whinney invaded the bedroom, bringing the conversation to an abrupt stop. Mory had forgotten Dancer. She rushed downstairs, leaping over Splodge, who sank to his tummy, dug his claws into the carpet and stared after his whirlwind mistress with flattened ears. What was she doing? It was bedtime and he was on his way to Mory's bed as any sensible cat should be.

"Sorry, Splodge," she cried, rushing into the

kitchen and out through the back door.

"Mory, where are you going? You've still got those wet clothes on."

"To turn Dancer out." Wellies on in a jiffy she was gone, out into the drizzly dampness. Dancer was hungry and impatient.

"Steady, steady, manners," said Mory. "I know you want to be with the others. Just wait."

Two pony faces looked over the paddock gate, Misty's grey and Rustler's chestnut one, ears pricked waiting for their friend. Mory pushed them back and led Dancer through, closing the gate behind her. She brought Dancer round to face the gate before slipping the halter off. As soon as she was free Dancer bounded off, the two geldings leaping after her into the night.

"Lunatics," said Mory delighted with their antics but knowing they would soon settle and eat. Crossing the yard she saw David silhouetted in the pottery window and poked her head round the door.

"Night, Dad." Stooping low David carefully put down a pile of sand-coloured bricks. "Hey, you've started building the new kiln."

"Certainly have," said her father, brushing dust from his hands, "and so far, it's going all right."

"No more temporary home. You'll soon be out of the cowshed," said Mory.

"Certainly will."

"Want some help to move the bricks?"

"Not tonight. You've got school in the morning and it's late."

"Okay."

Mory was thoughtful as she went indoors. Her dad nearly had a pottery. It was what he'd always dreamed of. It was funny how good things had happened because of moving. Josh had Rustler on trial, Cara wasn't lonely any more and Mum enjoyed supply teaching at Aberdawl Comprehensive. Dreams can come true. Well, hers had of owning Midnight Dancer. That was best of all.

Mory pulled off her wellies and wandered into the kitchen. Stretching her arms round her mother's neck she kissed her goodnight. Sheila responded absent-mindedly until the feel of damp fabric made her start.

"If you don't get those wet clothes off I'm going to pull them off personally," she said. "Do you want pneumonia?"

Mory sighed. What a fuss. She was perfectly warm and had no intention of getting pneumonia. Obediently she pulled off her sweatshirt and un-zipped her jeans. She hung them both on the airer above the oven range.

"Hot bath," said Sheila.

"Going."

Mory lay for ages in the warm bubbly water allow-ing her imagination to stretch ahead to Penyworlod Pony Show. Half term wasn't far away and they had the whole holiday week to practise before the show on the final Saturday. Mory wanted to enter Dancer for the dressage test and the handy pony competition. Dancer had proved she could jump with one brave leap but Mory thought it was probably too soon to enter the show jumping.

With a flicker of irritation Caroline Spencer spun into her thoughts. Caroline, who had mocked and disbelieved her when everyone else had believed. No one had seen the jump yet no one other than Caroline had called her a liar. But she hadn't lied. The jump was true.

Anger shattered Mory's reverie. She pulled out the plug and reached for a towel.

"Well, I'm not rushing things with Dancer just to prove to Caroline she can jump!" said Mory. The water swirled and gurgled as she towelled herself vigorously. She pulled on her pyjamas, forgot to clean her teeth and bumped into Josh on the landing.

"I've just thought," he said. "Old Mr Lewis's cottage."

"What about it?"

"The grey ghost!"

"But it's empty."

"Maybe it's not any more." The idea took root.

"Maybe it's not," she said. "We'll ride there tomorrow and find out."

Mory climbed into bed and gazed at the three drawings of Dancer done before the pony was hers.

Two photographs were pinned beside them of Mory riding Dancer for the first time. She badly wanted a third of Dancer jumping a huge jump which would be proof for ever that she could. Splodge curled across her feet and Mory let her fingers slip through his soft fur. She would draw Dancer's first jump. She remembered it clearly; she'd nearly fallen off. She let out a long sigh.

"I wish I was better at jumping. Dancer and I are as green as grass." Climbing out of bed she put her pastels ready on the table. Back under the duvet she wriggled her feet under Splodge and switched out the light. With another deep sigh she slid gently into sleep while Splodge purred in his favourite place.

# TWO

## *Stray*

The next morning Mory was up early mucking out Dancer's stable before school. She was interrupted by Cara's rapid arrival in the yard.

"Where's Josh?"

"Finishing breakfast. What's up?"

"Mab's had her puppies."

"Great! How many?" called Mory.

"Five," Cara replied and rushed indoors.

Josh was learning to work sheep with Mab, a keen, intelligent sheep dog, and was eager for these puppies. Uncle Glyn was proud of her.

"Best dog I've ever had," Uncle Glyn said. Josh wanted a dog like Mab and one of her puppies would be his best chance.

He tumbled into the yard, dragging his school rucksack and pulling on his anorak.

"I'm going to see the puppies," he called. "There's time before the bus."

"Are you coming?" Cara asked.

"Yes," Mory cried, flinging down the broom. "I'll catch you up. Where are they?"

"In the top barn."

Mory fled indoors, scattering her wellies, and grabbing her trainers. Her rucksack was in the hall.

"Don't forget your lunch-box," said David, tossing it to her. "Have you finished mucking out?"

"Nearly. I want to see the puppies."

"Just don't miss the bus!"

"We won't." Mory stuffed her lunch-box into her rucksack and ran.

She arrived at the top of the track puffing but with enough energy left to sprint across the Llangabby yard. The brittle brightness of the morning left her blinded as she tiptoed into the dimly lit barn letting her rucksack slip to the floor.

"Where are you?" she called softly.

"Over here," said Josh. "She doesn't mind us looking."

In the far corner, surrounded by bales of straw, Mab lay on her side with five tiny, helpless, black and white bundles between her legs.

"Oh, they're sweet," whispered Mory. "You clever girl." Mab acknowledged the compliment with a soft wag of her tail and with a mother's pride licked one of the puppies. Mory crouched beside Josh and Cara. So absorbed were they that they didn't hear Uncle Glyn arrive until he spoke.

"You'd better run," he said. "The bus is due in two minutes." He smiled at their reluctance. "They'll still be here when you get back."

Dragging themselves away they crept to the door, then fled across the yard. At the bottom of the lane they flung their bags at one another and laughed until the bus arrived. Josh rushed to join his friends at the back, eager to tell them about the puppies. Mory drew Cara to a seat on their own.

"Something weird happened last night when I was up on the ridge." Mory looked over her shoulder to make sure no one was listening, then told in a low voice about the leaping grey shape that had chased her and vanished in a moment.

"Can only have been a dog," said Cara. "Unless it was a mad ram!" She laughed but was suddenly serious. "If there is a loose dog we'd better tell Dad."

"Why?"

"In case it chases the sheep."

"Of course," said Mory. "But it wasn't alone. I'm sure it was called off. Don't say anything to Uncle Glyn. Not yet. We don't know it's done any chasing and we can try and find out about it after school."

"If there is a rogue dog Dad'll want to be rid of it."

"*If* there is," said Mory.

They didn't have time to discuss it any further as the bus drew up outside Llantrist Village School, their school. Mory enjoyed coming here and had got used to its smallness. The juniors were in one class, the infants in the other. It made the school she used to go to seem huge.

They tumbled into the playground in time to see the red-headed Lionel Jones putting his bike in the bike shed. Mory gave him a wave. He raised a hand in reply. Mory was sorry that Lionel seemed to have such a rough time, what with a most unlikeable dad and Caroline Spencer digging at him whenever she could. Mory was convinced Caroline was jealous because Lionel could ride her precious Elveston Tawney better than she could but that was no reason to be so horrid.

Caroline waltzed across the playground swinging her pink bag. The smirk she gave Lionel made Mory's hackles rise. Caroline had only to say one word. For once she didn't say anything, just lifted her nose in the air, before pushing her way into school. The others followed leaving Mory to wait for Lionel.

He came out of the bike shed and after him came

a shaggy, grey dog. Mory could only stare. The resemblance to the darting grey shape on the ridge was astonishing. It could have been the same dog if it hadn't been so much smaller. Lionel grinned shyly at her surprise.

"Whose is that?" Mory asked.

"Don't know. Found him," said Lionel. "Adopted me, 'e 'as." Lionel looked pleased. "Might have been left by holiday people."

"You mean on purpose?"

"'Spect so. Some people do." Mory was scandalized.

"How could they?" Lionel shrugged, accepting that people did cruel and irresponsible things.

"He's not old. Under a year. Could have grown too big or something," said Lionel, pulling one of the dog's floppy ears affectionately. "I like him. He's nice. I shall keep him."

"And your dad doesn't mind?" Lionel looked at Mory as if she had just said the daftest thing in the world and shook his head.

"Going to leave him at Penyworlod. Megan and Ian say I can."

Of course, thought Mory, of course they would. Once again she was reminded of how kind the Reeces were. They had helped her with Dancer and now they would help Lionel with the dog. Lionel, the best rider she knew. Megan and Ian taught him and now they were teaching her too. Talk of the Reeces reminded her that a lesson was booked for the following

Saturday. Her thoughts slipped to Dancer. She would jump properly then with Megan's help.

The dog reared up and put his front paws on Lionel's shoulders.

"What are you going to do with him?" asked Mory. "Bring him into school?" Lionel gave him a hug then pushed him off.

"Tie him in the bike shed. Come on, Ben." The dog followed obediently.

"How do you know his name?"

"That's what I call him. He learned it quick," said Lionel.

In the bike shed Lionel got out a plaited rope made of baler twine. He tied it to the plaited twine collar Ben wore round his neck.

"Can I stroke him?" Mory asked.

"If you want. He's friendly enough." Mory ran her hand through Ben's straggly, grey fur finding the bumps of his spine and his prominent ribs.

"He's very thin."

"Starving," said Lionel. "Must have wandered a while. I'm feeding him up. Doing the rubbish tidying at the shop for Mrs Pugh. She gives me scraps. Sometimes a tin. And dog biscuits."

"What about the money you get working for Megan and Ian on Saturdays?"

"Dad gets that."

"All of it?" Lionel didn't reply, which was enough for Mory to know that he did. Mr Jones was a horrible man. But she had money. Next time her mother or father went shopping in Aberdawl she would go too. Poor Ben. He did look hungry.

The two of them followed the others into school, leaving Ben lying on guard beside the bike shed, and the morning progressed like any other. At playtime Lionel slipped into the bike shed without anyone noticing. Not even his friend Gareth seemed to know Ben was there. Mory mentioned the dog to no one. She'd let Lionel tell when he was ready.

It was lunchtime when the news broke and Ben became a celebrity. So many children wanted to see him that quite a crowd gathered in the bike shed.

"Let him off, Lionel," said Gareth. "Go on. We can't see him properly in here." Lionel, pink and proud under his red hair and freckles, undid the lead. Ben wriggled between the children and bounded across the playground. Admirers chased after him. Ben barked and, side-stepping neatly, ran back to Lionel.

"Good dog, good boy," Lionel said, rubbing Ben's head before the dog bounded round the playground for a second time. There were squeals of delight and some of fright from the smaller children. Ben was enjoying himself. A long blast on the school whistle brought everyone to a standstill, except Ben, who roamed confused. Mrs Price, their teacher's helper, stood firmly in the middle of the playground with Caroline Spencer triumphant beside her. Caroline had told. Mory could see that, but she knew a dog wouldn't be a secret for long. Ben slunk between the children and collapsed at Lionel's feet as if he knew that he was in trouble.

"How did that dog get in the playground?" demanded Mrs Price, advancing on the embarrassed Lionel.

"He's mine," said Lionel. "I brung him. I'll tie him up again."

"Tie him up where?"

"In the bike shed."

"Oh, no you won't. You'll put him out of the playground at once."

"No," said Mory under her breath. Mrs Price's face was unbending and severe. But she wasn't the teacher. Mrs Wynne was. Mrs Wynne would listen. Mory, disobeying the rule about not moving until the second whistle, raced into school and banged on Mrs Wynne's office door before bursting through like a thunderbolt. "Please," she said. "Please, don't let Mrs Price turn Lionel's dog out. Not onto the road. He might get run over or run away thinking Lionel doesn't want him any more."

Mrs Wynne stood up and not waiting for further explanation, followed Mory into the playground. They were met by an extraordinary sight. A half circle of children were gathered behind Lionel who was glaring up at Mrs Price, furious and defiant, and at his feet, ready to spring, was Ben, lip curled, daring this woman to touch his master.

"Now, now, what's all this about?" said Mrs Wynne, her soothing tone breaking the tension. Ben responded first with a bow and slight wag of his long shaggy tail.

"I'm not putting him in the road," said Lionel. "If he goes, I go."

Out of the corner of her eye Mory saw Caroline raise her eyebrows, patronising Lionel's daring. She could almost hear her whisper an exasperated – oh, really! Mory hated her for it.

"I didn't know you had a dog, Lionel. He looks a good friend."

"He is," said Lionel, still defiant, wondering which way the wind was blowing.

"But Mrs Price is quite right; we don't bring our pets to school."

"That's what I told him," said Mrs Price, her face locked and grim, her authority threatened.

"Maybe we can sort something out. Lionel, you come with me." Lionel hesitated. "Bring the dog. And Mrs Price, if you would come too?" Mrs Wynne led the way. Just before she went into school Mrs Price blew a brief blast on her whistle, unfreezing everyone and enabling the children to burst into chatter.

They were all on Lionel's side except Caroline, who didn't say anything. Very wise, Mory thought, under the circumstances. But Caroline still had that "I know better than you" smirk on her face.

With the time they had left Mory gathered her friends, Cara, Sarah and Josh. Gareth, Lionel's friend, joined them too.

"This is a secret. Promise you won't tell. Caroline mustn't find out. She's such a sneak. Mr Jones doesn't know about Ben. He'd never let Lionel keep him if he did. Right." She had their attention. "So let's save some of our lunches. Dogs love sandwiches. We could get extra. That way we'll help Lionel feed him. Lionel hasn't got much money for dog food. And Ben is such a lovely dog."

"Agreed," said Cara. They spat on their palms and shook on it. Mory felt better after that.

At the end of lunchbreak Mrs Price blew the whistle. She was less ruffled, more her normal self. Lionel and Ben did not appear. On the second blast they filed into school. Mory sat at the table she shared with Cara, Sarah, Caroline, Gareth and Lionel. When at last Lionel came in Mory wondered what Mrs Wynne had said and where Ben was but there was no chance to find out. Lionel wouldn't tell in front of the others.

The afternoon wore on with reading and writing and Mory's thoughts drifted to their evening ride. From the tall window she could see voluminous white clouds scattered across a pale sky. It would be the right sort of evening for an adventure. Her mind being elsewhere Mory was unprepared when Caroline casually let slip a nasty barb.

"My daddy's selling Elveston Tawney, you know," she said. "I don't want him any more." Mory glanced at Lionel knowing what Tawney meant to him, schooling him at the Reeces and everything. "Still Lionel, now you've got that mangy mongrel you won't mind not riding him any more, will you?" If Caroline expected some amazing howl she was disappointed. Lionel put a book in the plastic bag hanging from his chair as if he had not heard. But he had.

"The trouble with you is that you can't bear to see someone ride Tawney better than you," Mory said, furious on Lionel's behalf. "A plodder like Doughnut is more your mark." That was unfair and Mory knew it. Doughnut was a fine pony, just not as temperamental or as highly strung as Tawney. But Mory was angry. Cara, seeing the signs, put a hand on her cousin's arm. Accepting the warning Mory turned away. If she didn't watch it the day would end in a slanging match, a pointless, humiliating war of words. You could never win with Caroline. Her sharp tongue always wounded. To escape it Mory picked up her rucksack and left the classroom.

Fortunately, the school bus was waiting. She plonked herself on the nearest seat, overcome by a feeling of intense loathing. Caroline, seemingly unperturbed, crossed the playground and was greeted by her mother waiting at the gate. She swung her pink bag all the way to the car. Mory stared hatred then watched helplessly as Lionel came out of school and pedalled down the street with scruffy, long-haired Ben trotting meekly behind. She wondered what had happened about the dog but when the others arrived they didn't know. For a moment she was tempted to chase after Lionel to find out, but the bus would go without her. Bother! She would have to wait until tomorrow. She didn't have time for a long walk home when there was an important mystery to solve out on the hills.

# THREE

## *Jump*

Mory was brushing Dancer's tail when Cara poked her head over the stable door.

"I'm nearly ready, are you?"

"Yes," said Mory. "Where's Josh? He said he was coming with us."

"He is coming," said Cara. "He went to see the puppies. We'd better wait."

"Not for long," said Mory. "I want to get going."

Cara, used to Mory's impatience, didn't let it ruffle her and went to collect Misty's tack from the tack room. She missed her own little tack room when Misty was at Black Rock but was glad he was with friends. Cara swung her saddle onto the stable door and warned Misty not to knock it off. It was a relief to see Josh bound into the yard.

"Josh's here," she called, going into the stable to move the saddle in case Misty did give it a nudge. Mory poked her head out of Dancer's stable.

"Hurry up Josh or we're going without you."

"I'm going to change," he called running indoors.

When Misty was tacked up Cara fetched a head-collar. Still Josh didn't appear. Mory yelled that Josh had one more minute and that was that. Cara decided to fetch Rustler herself.

She found Rustler waiting patiently by the paddock gate. She put on his headcollar and led him to his stable. Mory, at feverpitch of frustration, watched Cara start grooming.

"It's all very well but why should *we* groom his pony?" she fumed.

"It's because of the puppies," said Cara. "He wanted to see them. And it's not *we* grooming Rustler, it's *me*."

"There won't be any time left to do anything at this rate. I can't be late again. I got it in the neck last night." Mory stomped off to fetch Rustler's tack, bumping into Josh on the way back.

"'Bout time too," she said, thrusting the saddle at him.

"I went to see the puppies!"

"I know, I know."

"Uncle Glyn says there are two females and three males. He's keeping the two females. One for me and one for him. He's going to sell the others."

"Fine, just hurry up." Mory pushed him into Rustler's stable where Josh told Cara all over again.

"Look, I'm getting going," said Mory. "I'll meet you on the ridge by the rocks. Okay?" And she pulled on her hat. In Dancer's stable she unhooked the reins from underneath the stirrups where they had been looped for safety and led the pony out. She tightened the girth and looked up. A car was coming down the track. Their car bringing Sheila home from Aberdawl.

"Where are you off to?" her mother asked as she drew up. David came from the pottery no doubt to ask the same question.

"For a ride. The others are coming too."

"But where?"

"Up on the ridge and back," said Mory. "We won't be long. The weather's fine today," she added as if that made everything all right.

"No longer than an hour," said David.

"Okay," said Mory glancing at her watch. She was getting fed up with being mollycoddled. Mounting she turned to go.

"I thought you said you were going with the others," Sheila said.

"I am. They're following me up."

As if to prove the point Josh led out Rustler and Cara fetched Misty. Dancer set off leaving the others to catch up. David and Sheila exchanged looks. Cara and Josh mounted quickly.

"You heard that you two. Only an hour."

"Yes," said Cara. "We're only going for a little hack." She felt deceitful knowing what they were really going to do. But grown-ups did worry so.

"Bye," said Josh with a wave and the two of them followed Mory out of the yard.

Dancer walked purposefully down the track to the sheep path, her rider full of determination. The others wanted to catch up but the track was too stony to go fast. Mory trotted up the narrow sheep path. The going was good, not too soft after yesterday's rain. She let Dancer break into a canter. The pony took off up the hill, twisting and turning, arriving at the top eager to go on. Mory slowed so the others could catch up. She took in the view. Here was freedom in this vast space where the earth met the sky, where sheep were scattered cotton wool puffs against the heather and a buzzard mewed.

Mory drank in the landscape until something caught her eye. Something loping towards the rock crop on the high point of the ridge. Even from this distance she could see it was a large dog. Several alarmed sheep took to their heels. Ignoring them the dog loped on, unhurried but purposeful, until it disappeared from view. Voices and the thud of hooves distracted her.

"Quick!" Mory shouted. "I've seen it." She urged Dancer into a canter. "Go on," she said. Dancer, delighted, galloped flat out along the ridge. The others thundered behind her. Approaching the rocks Mory slowed to a canter, to trot, to walk, and behind her the others did the same. They crept to the high point and looked down, the only sound the heavy breathing of the ponies.

Mory's quick eyes scanned the heather. Nothing.

Three riders silhouetted themselves against the skyline before following the ridge and descending to the dip in which nestled Old Mr Lewis's cottage.

They came in a line as if observing a secret together. The old stone cottage, still and quiet amongst the apple trees, gave nothing away. What couldn't be hidden was a green Range Rover parked by the broken gate and a thin trickle of smoke rising from the chimney.

"Someone is here," said the smoke.

"Yes, someone is here," said the faded, used Range Rover. The house was on watch; someone was there.

Mory shivered. It was the strangest feeling. They looked at one another, unsure.

"Well," Mory said. "There's no reason why we shouldn't be here. I bet that's where the dog comes from. Let's go down and say hello." Doubt was written all over Josh and Cara. "Well at least we can go and see if the dog is there. Then we'll know where it belongs." Mory wanted to know. Someone was living in the cottage, someone who hadn't said hello at either Llangabby Farm or Black Rock, the only neighbours before miles of wild lonely hills. Her curiosity to find out was stronger than the strange feeling which said *keep away*.

"Tell you what, you stay here and keep watch. I'll do a recce."

Mory turned Dancer off the track and skirted the top of the dip crunching across the heather. The going was rough and she gave Dancer plenty of rein, letting the pony drop her head low in order to see. They followed a sheep path towards the silent cottage. Down they went. There was no dog and no people. She lost sight of Josh and Cara when the sheep track petered out. Then she saw them against the skyline, waiting.

Mory was close now and vulnerable. Suddenly her courage failed and she rode Dancer towards the main track. Too late! There was a deep bark and the large grey dog leapt from the garden sniffing the air. Mory turned away in a panic. The movement caught the dog's eye and it bounded forward. Snorting, Dancer sprang to escape. The huge, fallen trunk of an oak tree lay straight across their path. Mory gasped when she saw it but there was no stopping now. Out of the

corner of her eye she saw the riders on the ridge. Distracted, she miscounted the strides. One, two, and before she knew it Dancer was in the air. Caught out, Mory could do nothing but let herself fall and she hit the ground with a sickening thud – every bit of breath knocked from her.

She lay rigid as Dancer's galloping hooves receded. She couldn't breathe. Blood rushed in her ears and still she couldn't breathe. It was awful. At last there was a horrid rasping noise as her lungs began to fill and she was snatching great breaths in blissful relief. In, out. In, out. Not moving, just breathing.

Something wet licked her ear, then her cheek. A long tongue draped itself across her forehead. She tried to brush it aside but it was insistent.

"Get off," she grunted and would have laughed

except it hurt. "You're drowning me." She looked up into the huge, shaggy face of the grey dog. It sat back and lifted a paw. At first Mory thought it wanted to shake hands and then realized it seemed to be pointing her out, for behind the dog stood a gaunt lady in a tweed suit and wellies with a look of severity that Mory interpreted as trouble. She tried to get up but it was too soon.

"Winded are you?" asked the lady. That must be it thought Mory and managed to roll over. "Wait until you're ready."

"I'm fine," said Mory, not feeling it. "Where's Dancer? Where are the others?"

"If you mean your pony, Hector scared it off." Mory struggled to her feet.

"Don't worry," said the lady. "It will have gone straight home. They usually do you know. You'll have to walk. If you can that is?"

Everything spun and Mory swayed against the amiable dog, holding his fur until the world was still again.

"Your pony's got quite a jump in her. I'm not surprised you came off. She turned this log into a five-bar gate."

"You saw her?" Mory asked. The lady didn't reply and Mory realized she had been watching all along. She must have let the dog out to scare her off. But he wasn't scary now. He was soft and kind and loveable. She felt confused.

"Did you bang your head?"

"I don't know."

"Where do you live?"

"At Black Rock Farm." The lady's expression remained fixed and Mory felt obliged to go on. "Down the track from Llangabby Farm. You pass Llangabby to come onto the hills." There was an uncomfortable pause.

"I've seen the track," said the lady. "It's not so very far." She gave Mory a searching look. "I think I'd better take you home in the car."

"No," said Mory. "No, please, I'm fine now. Really." She didn't want David and Sheila to find out that she had fallen off. Struggling with her cuff she looked at her watch. She had twenty minutes to find Dancer, find the others and get back. "Thank you very much all the same." She backed away. "I'm glad he doesn't chase sheep, your dog. He's nice."

"Whatever made you think he would do that?" It did seem unlikely. Hector was well trained, Mory could see that as he sat patiently by his mistress, his nose touching her hand.

"Goodbye," Mory said to cover her confusion.

"Goodbye," said the lady. She seemed amused. Mory couldn't think why.

"I hope you'll be very happy here. It's beautiful out on the hills," she said impulsively. Unexpectedly, the lady smiled.

"Thank you," she said. "I'm sure I shall."

Mory ran stumbling up the sheep path, not looking back, feeling stupid. She had lost Dancer. She hoped the lady was right and that Dancer had gone straight home. Puffing hard with a growing ache in her arm she reached the ridge. Not far now to the rocks. No Dancer in sight. She stumbled on, up and up, her breath coming in harsh, heaving pants and saw them. Three ponies and two riders coming towards her. The relief was overwhelming.

"That's all that matters." Tears pricked her eyes. "Dancer is safe." She slumped against the hard stone and waited, her energy spent.

The others trotted on when they saw her, arriving, stirrups chinking, anxious, concerned.

"Are you all right?" said Cara. "The lot of them bolted."

"We saw the dog," said Josh. "It was huge."

"I'm fine," said Mory. At least she thought she was. She flexed her fingers. Her arm was stiffening. "I was winded and I've bashed my arm, that's all. Is Dancer all right?"

"What happened?" Cara asked. "Why did you fall off?"

"Didn't you see?"

"All we saw was Dancer going like mad. Ours just spun and went with her. We let them go in case the dog came too," said Cara lamely. "We didn't try and stop them for ages."

Something clicked in Mory's brain.

"Was there a whistle?" she asked.

"There might have been," said Josh. "The dog didn't follow us."

"The lady said it was trained. I don't think it would have chased anything without being told to. I think she meant to frighten us."

"What lady?" said Cara. Mory heaved herself onto Dancer's back.

"The lady who's moved into the cottage," she said and told them about the dog called Hector and Dancer's "five-bar-gate" jump. They listened wide-eyed.

"Wow!" said Cara. "Some jumping pony."

"She is," said Mory giving Dancer an affectionate pat. "Quick, we've ten minutes before we're due back. Don't let's be late." And she led the way fast along the ridge for home.

# FOUR

## *Do It Again*

Mory sat in Dancer's stable with her arm in the water bucket. It was numb with cold but this seemed a good way to try and stop the bruise.

"Better than a break," said Cara.

"Too right! I wouldn't be able to do the Penyworlod Show."

"Let's have a look." They scrutinized the dripping limb. On the under side was a purple swelling.

"Must have landed on a stone," Mory said. She gave it a rub and pulled her sleeve down. "That'll do."

"Do you think the lady has come to live here for good?" Cara mused.

"I don't know. She's strange, kind of old and stiff. And she's got a posh voice. She knew we were spying."

"We weren't spying," said Cara. "We were checking on the dog to see if it chased sheep, remember?"

"It didn't. I'd already seen it ignore some sheep. I wanted to find out who was in the house. That's spying."

Josh leaned over the stable door.

"Food's ready," he said and, message delivered, departed again.

"Better go in."

"Put a bandage on. To stop it swelling," advised Cara.

"It's not that bad," said Mory. Cara shrugged.

They stopped by the paddock gate and contemplated the ponies grazing amiably side by side. It occurred to Mory that if Dancer ran off every time she saw Hector this might not be the only time she fell off.

"I wish you'd seen the jump, Cara. I wish you had."

"So do I," said Cara. "I bet it was brilliant." Mory sighed. Caroline Spencer would never believe it. Not if no one had seen it. She wished she didn't mind so much.

"Are you going to eat with us?"

"I told Mum I'd be back," said Cara. "I'd better go."

"Love to everyone and a pat to Mab," said Mory, remembering the puppies.

As she went indoors an uncomfortable feeling took root inside her. Something to do with the lady and David and Sheila not approving of what she had done. Worse still, the lady had seen her fall off. If her parents met her, she hoped the lady wouldn't mention it. She gave her arm a squeeze. The bruise wasn't that bad. She decided to forget about it and sent out a wish that the lady would forget about her too.

There was a welcoming cooking smell in the kitchen.

"Did you have a good ride?" Sheila asked.

"Yes, thanks," Mory said. She caught Josh's eye.

"It was great," said Josh. "We had a fantastic gallop and you'll never guess …!" Mory glared at him in the pause that followed. "We got home in record time." He grinned. Mory narrowed her eyes at him.

"Not too fast I hope," said Sheila. "I don't want any accidents."

"We were fine, Mum," said Mory, aiming a secret dig. Expecting it Josh slid away. Mory was not in the mood to be teased.

"Now, now, you two," said David. "Stop mucking about and take this." He handed Mory a plate. She gave Josh a final glare and sat down. She was hungry and ate steadily letting her mind wander, not listening to Josh's chatter about Mab and the puppies. Slowly a picture formed. The jumping picture she had waited all day to draw.

When the washing up was done Mory went upstairs. She sat and stared at the blank paper ready on her table. Absent-mindedly opening her pastels box she saw Dancer gallop across the page, mane and tail flying, towards the fallen oak. This time she counted one, two, three strides and Dancer took off, powerful hocks under her, soaring in a graceful arc to a perfect landing before cantering on.

Mory chose the black pastel and with a flowing

gesture drew a line across the clean white page. Slow at first, her hand moved here and there, head, mane, tail, legs, Dancer in the air. She reached for another colour. The oak tree, fallen, broken, roots exposed. She saw it all, her hand speeding to capture everything. And herself, high, leaning into the jump, at one with the pony and the great leap.

At last she sat back satisfied and returned the pastels one by one to their box. The picture was her dream; the reality – herself a winded heap on the ground. A furry bundle wound itself around her legs and let out a sad little mew. Mory gathered Splodge up and cuddled into the softness of his fur.

"If only I hadn't fallen off," she whispered. Splodge purred. "This is a secret, Splodge. I'm going to jump the fallen tree again. By myself." Splodge curled into a ball. He wouldn't think of telling and neither would she. Then no one could stop her.

Gently she lowered Splodge to the bed and picked up the picture. She'd got it just right. Deciding on the place, Mory pinned this pinnacle of her ambition above the others on the wall.

Next morning at school Mory waited for Lionel. It was irritating that Caroline arrived first, swinging her pink bag. Mory ignored her, eyes on the gate. The pink bag swung closer. Mory moved away. Caroline moved with her, swinging and swinging until the bag brushed Mory's leg. With the next swing Mory grabbed it.

"Give me my bag!" Mory was stronger than Caroline had expected and her eyes flickered, unsure. There was no one to help. Mory held the bag just long enough, said nothing and let go. Caroline swung the bag away and with a toss of her head pushed her way into school.

In her imagination Mory kicked the offending bag all over the playground until it was no longer pink but a dirty brown. But when Lionel's head showed above the wall she quickly forgot about it. His brakes squealed and he came to a dead stop in front of the gate, back wheel in the air. A quick leg over flip and he was on his way in, followed by Ben, tongue lolling, panting from his run.

"You got him?" Mory grinned with pleasure.

"From Penyworlod."

"Surely Megan and Ian would keep him there?"

"When do I get to see him then? Only after school and on Saturdays. Mrs Wynne says I can. He's to stay in her office."

"Great," said Mory. She knew Mrs Wynne would help.

"I get to see him lunch-time that way."

"We're going to help feed him," said Mory, stroking Ben's head.

"Who is?" said Lionel, suspiciously.

"Me, Cara, Josh, Gareth, Sarah."

"Not her?"

"No, not Caroline. She doesn't know anything."

"Don't tell her but Megan and Ian are buying Tawney. It's to sell on."

"Do you mind?"

"Not really. There's other horses. And I got Ben." He patted the dog who lifted up trusting eyes.

"Here, Mory, put his lead on will you?"

Mory took the baler twine rope and tied it to Ben's collar.

"He's to be on the lead all the time he's in school. If he's off he's out. That's what Mrs Wynne said."

They walked to the bike shed. Other children coming into school patted the shaggy, grey dog who wagged his tail at each greeting.

"Lionel," said Mory. "When approaching a jump, what's the most important thing to do?" Lionel swung his bike into a rack and unclipped his polythene bag.

"To see the stride, to get it right for the horse. If it comes in right it can get over. And rhythm. To keep the rhythm. That's what Megan says. She uses poles for that." Mory groaned. She knew there would be more to it than just sitting there and counting. "You hold the horse together so it jumps with its hocks under, nice and round. Once you get your eye in it's not so hard."

"Only yesterday Dancer jumped this log and I fell off."

"Jumped it big I expect," said Lionel. "Well, she will, she's not used to jumping. Neither are you. It's practice."

"I suppose you're right."

"Jump it again. Once she's used to it she'll jump as much as she needs, no more, she's not daft."

They went into school and Lionel with Ben at his side knocked on Mrs Wynne's office door. Armed with this new information Mory went to hang up her coat. She sat on the bench in the cloakroom and pondered the advice. She was still sitting there when Lionel came to hang up his jacket. He slung his bag over his shoulder and looked awkwardly at his feet.

"What you need is help," he said, "with the jumping."

"Yes, I know but it's sort of secret. I just want to be able to … to well, show everyone I can." Lionel looked up. "Stay on," Mory added.

"Everyone falls off. I do."

"You do?"

"If I make a mistake. Sometimes the pony does something daft. I've been off Tawney."

"You have?"

"Yes, I don't tell *her* that's all."

"You see I want to go back after school and jump the log by myself without anyone trying to stop me."

"The oak down by Hill Farm? I seen it," said Lionel. "Nice jump. Inviting."

"Hill Farm?"

"You lot call it old Mr Lewis's cottage. Give you a hand if you like?"

"After school?"

"Sure. After I been to the shop," he said. "I'll be there."

"Here," said Mory rummaging in her rucksack. She took out some sandwiches wrapped in a plastic bag. "Chicken ones. For Ben." Lionel went pink. "It's all right, honestly." He took them and went hurrying across the hall to the classroom.

After school Mory pounded into the Black Rock yard, breathless from her run down the track, intent on tacking up Dancer and going. In her haste she almost ran into her mother putting a bundle of empty shopping bags into the back of the car.

"Oh, good," said Sheila. "You've time for a quick drink and a piece of cake. The sooner we get going the better."

"Get going where?" said Mory, taken aback.

"To Aberdawl. To buy you new trainers. Those are a disgrace." Mory looked at her feet.

"What's wrong with them?"

"Don't tell me you've forgotten. We discussed it at breakfast." Something stirred in Mory's memory. "Now hurry up and get ready."

Mory wanted to run and hide. Pointless. Sheila wouldn't go without her. All day she had built up to jumping the fallen oak and now she couldn't. It was too bad. She sort of remembered about the new trainers but it hadn't sunk in that her mother meant to buy them tonight. What was she to do? Lionel would be waiting. Maybe if they were quick.

"How long's it going to take?"

"As long as it does."

"Let's go then," said Mory, flinging herself in the car. "I'm ready."

"Don't you want any cake? Okay, I'll just tell Dad we're off." Sheila headed in the direction of the pottery.

"Oh, hell's bells," said Mory and slumped into a heap. A horrid feeling told her that this was going to take for ever.

# FIVE

## *Challenge*

The excitement about jumping had completely evaporated by the time they drove back from Aberdawl. Time had run out. Buying trainers! Sheila hadn't said anything about spending hours going round the supermarket and getting stuck in the longest queue in the world. The day was over. The only good thing were the two large tins of dog food bought with a wheedled advance on her pocket money. They would go some way to make up for Lionel's wasted journey. She would give him them tomorrow when they went for their lesson at Penyworlod.

Mory cheered up at the thought. She may not have jumped the fallen oak but tomorrow she would jump in her riding lesson. Her foot nudged her rucksack feeling the weight of the tins. Enough food to keep Ben for days.

At last the car turned into the lane. Mory looked at her watch. Not even time to ride in the field.

"I'm sorry," said Sheila. "It's always busy on a

Friday and today couldn't have been worse." A morose reply died on Mory's lips, for the final bend in the lane revealed the Range Rover she had seen outside old Mr Lewis's cottage, or Hill Farm as Lionel called it. For some reason Uncle Glyn's Land-rover was barring its way and Uncle Glyn was gesticulating angrily at the lady inside. Sheila was forced to stop, there was no room to pass. Mory unclipped her seat belt.

"Don't interfere," said Sheila, putting out a restraining hand.

"Don't tell me that dog doesn't chase sheep," roared Uncle Glyn. "I saw it with my own eyes. I've got ewes and lambs up there." He pointed vehemently towards the hills. Hector stood in the back of the Range Rover with hackles raised and teeth bared.

"When did you see the dog?" the lady asked, her manner dignified and quiet.

"An hour back."

"He wasn't there," the lady said gently. "He was with me, in the back of the car while I went shopping."

"Pah!" exclaimed Uncle Glyn, not believing a word of it. "I'm warning you, I don't go up there again without my gun." He pulled something from his pocket. "If I catch him this is what he gets." He waved whatever it was under the woman's nose. A chill crept up Mory's spine. Uncle Glyn's hand held bullets!

"That won't be necessary," said the lady. "My dog is kept under control at all times. Now if you would kindly move your Landrover I would like to get home."

There was nothing else for it. The Landrover's engine roared and the vehicle swung violently into the farmyard. Now she could go forward the lady drove the Range Rover slowly across the cattle grid and sedately along the track to Hill Farm.

Mory found she had been holding her breath and slowly let it out. She had never seen her uncle so angry.

"Goodness!" said Sheila. "What on earth was that all about?"

It was obvious to Mory. Uncle Glyn thought Hector had been chasing sheep. But Mory knew he ignored sheep even when they ran from him. An awful thought turned her stomach. Ben! He would have been up on the hills an hour ago, with Lionel, waiting for her! At a distance it would be easy to mistake Ben for Hector. The same shaggy grey coat, the long greyhound shape. They did look strikingly similar.

The car bumped down the track with Mory pulling at her lip thinking the worst.

"Do up your seat belt," said Sheila. Automatically Mory did as she was told. She must warn Lionel or it might be Ben who was shot.

In a daze she carried two shopping bags indoors,

dumping them on the table. Sheila tossed her the carrier with the trainers in.

"Take them upstairs," she said and opened the fridge. "Oh, no! Who's been at this chicken?" Mory vanished fast.

Upstairs Mory tried the trainers on. They were neat. She liked the blue stripe down the sides and the comfortable cushioned soles. She jogged round the room and took them off again. Then quickly changed from her school things into her jeans. At least she could give Dancer a groom before tea.

There were hurrying feet on the stairs and Josh burst in, flushed and excited.

"Guess what," he said. "That lady's dog *has* been chasing sheep. Uncle Glyn saw it. He gave her a heck of a telling off."

"I know," said Mory. "Mum and I got stuck behind them. We heard it."

"What did he say?"

"He said he saw the dog chasing sheep. Then he pulled out bullets and said the dog would get them if he caught it doing it again." Mory paused. "It was horrid."

"But Mory …"

"It wasn't Hector. We know he doesn't chase sheep. Besides, he was with the lady. She had him in the back of the Range Rover while she went shopping."

"Her name's Mrs Ashfield."

"How do you know?"

"She bought eggs off Aunt Olwen."

"Don't s'pose she'll buy any more. Not after what Uncle Glyn said."

"Don't be daft. It's just Uncle Glyn doesn't want dead sheep."

"He hasn't got any dead sheep." At least Mory hoped that he hadn't. She was desperate to check with Lionel. Until then she was saying nothing.

The next day Mory was up bright and early. She scampered downstairs into the kitchen after Splodge and flung open the fridge door, looking for the opened tin of cat food. She found it behind the chicken carcass – a sore point with her mother.

"Here, Splodge," she said. Mory forked out fishy food into his bowl and unlocked the back door, putting the bowl in the porch. Splodge settled himself into a comfortable eating position and tucked in.

Mory's next chore was to clean her tack. A boring job but it had to be done. It was stiff and hard from the soaking it had had. She wondered if she could finish it before breakfast. Spurred on by the thought of food, she got stuck in and soaped away as hard as she could. She was lucky. The shout for breakfast came at just the right moment. Both saddle and bridle were done. The bridle was back together and hung neat and supple with a gleaming bit. Clean tack was always worth the effort in the end. By the time the second call came she had even tidied up.

"Coming!" she shouted and stood back for a moment to admire her handiwork, then hurried to the kitchen.

After breakfast Josh helped bring the ponies in and when Cara arrived they groomed and tacked them up ready to load in the trailer. Mory was so looking forward to the jumping part of the lesson. She imagined it as they led the ponies up the track to Llangabby, her school bag slung on her back heavy with dog food. She imagined it as Aunt Olwen drove them to Penyworlod in the Landrover. It was all she could think about – today she would jump Dancer!

The first person they saw when they turned into the car park was Caroline Spencer leading Doughnut behind the indoor school. As usual she was dressed in her smart hacking jacket, black boots and britches with her shiny velvet hat. Mory felt a twinge of envy. She would never be able to afford expensive clothes like that even though she had saved all her hard-earned money, the money from helping David with the pottery. She would have to buy second-hand riding clothes from the tack shop that Megan and Ian ran. But at least that would be better than jeans and wellies.

Aunt Olwen brought the Landrover to a gentle stop and everyone tumbled out. The front ramp was lowered and the ponies were led out.

"Hats," said Aunt Olwen. Cara, who was always

forgetting hers, flung Misty's reins at Mory and scrabbled in the Landrover. Josh fiddled with his chin strap while Mory did hers up. "All set? Then off you go."

Mr Spencer and Aunt Olwen followed, chatting amicably together. As they came round the indoor school Mory's eyes skimmed every nook and cranny for Lionel. He must be up by the stables, she thought, hoping he would put in an appearance soon.

Megan held Doughnut while Caroline mounted. Mory prepared to do the same. She tightened Dancer's girth and pulled down the stirrups. Standing on the near side she drew the reins into her left hand and turned the stirrup. Lifting her foot to it she sprang, letting the stirrup take her weight as she swung her leg over and sank lightly into the saddle. Her offside foot found its place and she was ready. She stroked Dancer's neck, a thank you for standing quietly.

"Come along," called Megan and led the way into the outdoor school.

The lesson proceeded as usual with walk, trot and canter. Canter! It was like everything. Mory thought she'd got it and then found there was more to it. You were supposed to get your pony to canter on the correct leading leg which was the inside front foreleg when going round in a circle. At first Mory had had no idea when she was wrong except that circling would feel a bit bumpy and Megan would shout. "Wrong leg, Mory."

Mory would look down and see that Dancer was leading with the offside foreleg and not the inside. In her determination to get it right she had spent hours imagining the canter aids – sit up, inside leg on the girth, outside leg behind, more weight on the outside seat bone, give and take with the inside rein. Prepare all that and ask. Now she was more certain of what she was doing Dancer seemed to understand better, so that more often than not they got it right.

"Mory!" It was her turn. "I want you to go to the edge of the school on the left rein, trot at E and at A canter in a twenty-metre circle until I tell you to stop," said Megan.

Mory walked Dancer from the line of ponies to the edge of the school. This was another thing she found confusing. The marker letters round the edge. She could remember them when she said to herself *A Fat Bat Made Cats Hate Elephants' Kicks.* She had thought up the words herself to help. A F B M C H E K was difficult on its own. But the words weren't much use when she was cantering because the letters whizzed by so fast. What she could remember was that A was opposite to C at the short ends and that B was opposite to E and X was in the middle. She had to look for the others. Thank goodness for the clear white letters.

E was coming up and she prepared to trot.

"A bit late," said Megan. "But a nice transition."

Mory trotted past K and turned the corner. She

prepared to canter by sitting to the trot and with her nearside leg on the girth she turned Dancer's head slightly, took her weight to the offside seat bone and brought her offside leg back, sat up and asked.

To her delight the rhythm changed and Dancer cantered along the line of a twenty-metre circle. Mory concentrated like anything to make the sides of the circle round and to hit the invisible X spot as she turned and turned. It felt smooth and fluid as though they could keep it up for hours.

"And trot, Mory," said Megan. "And walk. Very nice. You're tending to let everything go a bit at the front when you first ask but it's coming. Well done."

Mory gave Dancer a pat.

"We're getting it girl," she said, "we're getting it."

At the edge of the school Lionel watched but when Mory caught his eye he turned away. She wanted to call after him but couldn't in the middle of a lesson. Shoulders drooping he trudged towards the stables. With a pang Mory thought how let down he must feel about yesterday.

He had almost disappeared when Megan called him. He turned, shading his eyes against the sun.

"Can you help put up the jumps?" she asked. Lionel trudged back and handed in jump stands. He dragged poles to where Megan directed. There were to be three jumps that went jump stride jump stride jump. Megan put out two marker poles before the first jump which she measured out in strides. But there were no poles on the second and third jumps yet. They lay ready alongside. The riders put their stirrups up three holes to shorten them for jumping and were ready.

"Right," said Megan. "Who's going first?"

"I will," said Mory. "We jumped the other day by mistake."

"How did you get on?"

"Not very well. I fell off."

There was a splutter from Caroline.

"She jumped big," said Lionel, his eyes glancing at Caroline but telling Megan.

"Let's start her off with a lead," said Megan. "Cara, you take Misty over and round, and Mory, keep Dancer at least three lengths behind and follow Misty. Just at a trot, Cara. If Dancer canters after the jump, don't worry." Megan turned the first jump into a cross pole so it had a nice low inviting middle. The poles on the ground in front would help Dancer to get her stride right and Mory to see the stride.

Cara trotted Misty in a circle and, concentrating madly, Mory trotted after her. Cara approached the jump. Trot, trot, trot jump. It was nothing to an old hand like Misty. Dancer went eagerly forward after her friend. Trot, trot, trot jump. And they had done it.

"Give her a pat, Mory," said Megan, "and go round again."

Dancer trotted happily after Misty. Trot trot trot jump. They had done it again.

"This time on your own, Mory." Round they went again while Misty and Cara stayed at the far end of the school. Dancer pricked her ears. Trot trot trot jump. This time after the jump she burst into canter and her back rounded.

"Hold her head up, she's going to buck," called Megan. Too late! Dancer's hind legs shot up and Mory went flying. Megan hurried over to her while Lionel caught Dancer. Mory was on her feet in no time, quite unhurt but rather surprised.

"What did she do that for?" she asked.

"Pleased with herself," said Lionel leading Dancer over.

"Now," said Megan, concerned, "are you happy to go again? Because she's not used to jumping she's finding it rather exciting." Mory was already back in the saddle. "We'll give her something to think about. Lionel, put in a cross pole and make a second jump will you? And Mory, this time it will be jump, stride jump. Don't worry about it. And Lionel, take those extra jump stands away, please. Now Mory, after the second jump turn her so she can't buck so easily and when you've jumped both jumps sit up again. Don't stay leaning forward in the jumping position."

All was ready. Mory trotted Dancer in a circle and then faced the line of jumps. Dancer's ears pricked. Trot trot trot jump stride jump. After the second jump Mory sat up and turned Dancer. They cantered in a circle. The pony shook her head but Mory, forewarned of a buck, didn't give an inch.

"Very well done!" Megan's voice rang in her ears. A thrill spread through Mory. It didn't matter a bit that she had fallen off. She had done it.

It was Mory's turn to watch. Caroline was more confident riding Doughnut. Doughnut flew over the jumps, Rustler and Misty the same.

"We'll practise in the field and we *will* go back to the fallen oak. We will," she promised herself and Dancer.

"That was good." The voice beside her was unexpected.

"Lionel! About last night," she said. "Mum made me go shopping with her. I couldn't get out of it. I'm really sorry."

"Yeah."

"Look, I've got to talk to you. Only I don't want the others to know. Can you come to us before going home?"

"Bring Ben for a run."

"No, don't bring Ben. That's what I've got to tell you about. I'll meet you at the end of our lane, at the lay-by, where the bus stops."

"Six o'clock," said Lionel. "If I can." Mory laughed.

"Serve me right if you don't turn up," she said.

Their conspiratorial conversation over, Mory looked round to see Caroline trotting towards them.

"Well, Mory Harper, I suppose you think you can jump that thing now." Lionel grimaced.

"Lay off, Caroline, she's learning."

"And you can shut up for a start. I wasn't talking to you."

Cara and Josh, attracted by raised voices, led their ponies over. Fortunately, Megan and Aunt Owen talking by the gate hadn't heard.

"What's up?" Cara asked.

"I suppose you're all going to gang up on me now," said Caroline. "As usual."

"No one's ganging up on you," said Mory.

"You expect me to believe that?" said Caroline, swinging Doughnut round. "Next thing you'll be telling me is that Super Steed is going to be jumping at the show. Some hopes."

"Are you saying she couldn't?" said Mory, flaring up.

"Of course she couldn't. She can only jump titchy cross poles. She couldn't jump proper jumps. Not her." Mory caught Lionel's eye and he closed a lid in a slow, deliberate wink.

"Well I say she can."

"Okay, then prove it," said Caroline. "Enter her for the show jumping if you dare."

"I dare," said Mory. "I'll enter and what's more I'll win."

The words were out before she could stop them. *And I'll win* was going a bit far. But it was with some satisfaction that she watched Caroline flounce off. And she would enter Dancer for the show jumping and they would do their best to win if that's what it took to prove that Dancer was the fantastic pony she knew her to be.

# SIX

## *Entries*

Going home in the Landrover Mory sat with a Penyworlod Show entry form in her hand. What had she said? The words "I'll enter and what's more I'll win" were spinning over and over in her mind. Big mouth, she told herself. Enter yes, win – some chance. She let her eyes focus on the form and began to read it properly.

CLOSING DATE FOR ENTRIES 12TH MAY.

She worked out she had a week to decide on what to enter and a week to the show. Half term was only two weeks away!

"Do you think I can do it?" Mory asked.

"Do what?" said Cara, involved in a finger game with Josh.

"Get Dancer jumping well enough to enter the show. The beginners' class, what's it called, novice class."

"Dancer'll knock down all the jumps, cross her legs and refuse to finish," said Josh unhelpfully and burst into giggles.

"Thanks a bunch. I wasn't asking you."

"I think she'll jump really well if you practise," said Cara.

"But the show's only two weeks away."

"There's the half-term week before the show. Relax. You worry too much. Just practise. Dancer loves jumping. That's what all the head shaking and wanting to buck's about. Get her concentrating. Set her some challenges. Get her thinking about the next jump and not just having a good buck. She can do it."

"But can I?"

"Yes," said Cara. "Of course you can. The more you do the more confident you'll get."

"Are you talking about Dancer's jumping?" asked Aunt Olwen over her shoulder. "Megan was telling me what a lot of potential the pony's got. Thought she could go far."

"Go far?" said Mory leaning towards her aunt. "Megan said that?" Aunt Olwen laughed.

"I wouldn't be telling you otherwise."

"There," said Cara. "That would make Caroline Spencer green."

"Yuk," said Josh, pretending to be sick. "She's bad enough as it is, but green—" He made a revolting noise.

"Shut up, Josh," said Mory. "This is serious." Josh didn't agree. He made another repulsive noise and clutching his stomach rolled around his seat. Cara laughed.

"I've decided to enter for the show jumping," Mory informed Aunt Olwen.

"I gathered that," replied her aunt. "It'll give you something to work towards. That's always a good thing, I think." Then her aunt turned her attention to slowly swinging the Landrover into the farmyard. She did it neatly, born of long practice, coming to a halt by the barn.

Mory sat there for a moment while two things occurred to her. The first was that Dancer liked jumping and the second was that Caroline Spencer spoiled everything. So she would banish all thoughts of Caroline from now on and would please herself and her pony by doing lots of jumping. With that sorted out she jumped from the back door after the others.

"Here, Mory," said Aunt Olwen. "Don't forget this." And she handed Mory her rucksack. Inside two tins of dog food clunked together.

"Oh, no," said Mory. "I forgot to give ..." And she stopped. "Thanks, Aunt Olwen." She took the rucksack. It didn't matter. She would give Lionel Ben's food when she saw him later. She slung the bag on her back ready to help unload the ponies.

"So how was the lesson?" David asked when Mory reported for work in the pottery after lunch. She still didn't think she had enough money for jodhpurs, jodhpur boots and a hacking jacket, even second-hand.

"Really good," she replied. "We did jumping."

"So, it's up in the air stuff now, is it?" he teased.

"Up and down stuff," Mory corrected. "Oh, Dad, Dancer's wonderful."

"I know, the best pony in the whole world."

"She is. It's true. Don't be mean."

"Well, this pottery will be the best pottery in the whole world if I ever get it finished. Fancy some painting?"

"Painting what?"

"The back wall. I want it white to reflect as much light as possible. I've got lots of paint, brushes and a hat to keep the drips off. Here." He pulled an old pom pom hat onto Mory's head. "Very becoming," he said laughing.

"I bet I look stupid."

"Well, I can't say you don't." He flung some overalls in her direction. They were too big and David helped fold back the sleeves. "Right! I'll start at the top and do the up the ladder stuff. You do from where you can reach to the floor. Okay?" Mory nodded, dipped her brush in the thick white paint and spread a long glistening line across the red bricks. It was rather satisfying.

After an age, Mory's arm really ached. She put down the brush and looked at what she had done. She'd got about half way. David was faster and had passed her going the other way. A long strip of dark wall, hers to paint, stretched ahead while above it was bright white. But what was extraordinary was that it did make the pottery seem bigger.

"Tired?" asked David, balancing one-legged on his step-ladder.

"Arm ache."

"You've done well. Stop if you want."

Mory looked at her watch and thought of hacking jackets. No, she would go on. She would stop in time to meet Lionel. She changed hands and dipped the brush in the paint. She wasn't very good left-handed. The brush wobbled. Dipping the brush again she put it back in her right hand. Without meaning to a shape appeared, mane, ears, a head. A rearing white Dancer with kicking legs and flowing white tail. She put in a jump under the pony and then another further along the wall, arm ache forgotten. Jump stride jump replayed in her mind. She was so engrossed she didn't notice David get down.

"Seems a pity to paint over it," he said. Mory came to with a jolt.

"It's Dancer."

"I know." David put an arm round her shoulders and together they watched the vibrant white pony. But the paint had a life of its own and formed blobs. They ran in long rivulets and the picture lost its magic.

"I think I should buy a tin of black paint and let you paint me a real Dancer, say about here. And this big," said David. He stretched his arms from the back of the kiln to the drilled screw holes. "It's always fun to have a mural."

"Yes," said Mory, her eyes alight. "I could do it for your birthday. A mural birthday present."

"I should like that." David was pleased. "Come on, I'll help you finish."

Slowly the pony that was Dancer and the two jumps disappeared into whiteness. It was a relief to get to the end, and when they did Mory went to the sink and ran her brush under the tap.

"I've got to go now, Dad." David looked at his watch.

"Two hours, forty-five minutes. We can call it three." Mory grinned appreciation.

"Thanks, Dad." She struggled out of the overalls and pulled off the hat. "See you later." She flew out of the door across the yard to the tack room to retrieve her rucksack. Lionel was waiting by the time she got to the lay-by.

"I thought you might not come," she said, laughing. He stared at her face. "What's up?"

"You got white bits …" He pointed.

"Oh, it's paint. I've been helping Dad paint the pottery. Splashes."

"Your nose has a good one." He grinned. Mory rubbed it. "Still there."

"Never mind. Look, I got this for Ben." She pulled out the tins of dog food.

"No, I can't," said Lionel. "I can't take it."

"Look, you were going to help me with my jumping. It's not your fault I didn't turn up. I'm helping you with Ben in return. That's all. Seems fair to me."

"If we do go up Hill Farm. Fair dos."

"Tomorrow. Can you make a Sunday?"

"Suits me."

"About three o'clock? Don't come to Black Rock. I don't want the others to know. I want to surprise them. Meet you there?"

"Fine," said Lionel. He hesitated. "What's this you said about Ben?"

"Oh, Lionel." Mory wasn't sure how to put it. Accusing Ben of sheep chasing seemed horrid. But she had to find out. "When you were waiting yesterday, did Ben ... did he chase any of the sheep?" Lionel looked away.

"He had a go," he mumbled. "How d'you know?"

"Uncle Glyn saw." The story tumbled out in a rush. "He doesn't know it was Ben. He thinks it was the lady's dog. They look alike. She said it wasn't but Uncle Glyn didn't believe her. He was so angry. He had bullets and said he'd shoot the dog if he saw it chase sheep again. That means he'd shoot Ben too." Lionel nodded.

"Ben didn't do no damage. Honest. I called him off. It won't happen again. I swear."

"Can you train him?"

"'Course I can. I was stupid. I didn't expect him to

chase. He's been good so far, see." Lionel scuffed at the ground and kicked a pebble. "Bet the lady was upset."

"I don't know," said Mory. "I expect so. I was."

"I won't bring Ben," said Lionel. "He won't come 'til I'm sure of him. Okay?" Mory nodded.

Lionel, who'd been clutching the dog food to his chest, put it down by his bike and unclipped a polythene bag from the carrier. He added the tins. Climbing astride he swung the bike round.

"See you tomorrow then," he said, his gaze resting on the handlebars. "Thanks for telling me."

Mory rubbed the paint blob on her nose.

"I'd better get this off," she said. Lionel looked up and a grin flickered on his face before he pedalled off.

After supper Mory sat in her room looking at the show entry form and felt her courage fail. Jumping – Class 1 Novice. Jumps not to exceed 2 feet. How high was that? Her own ruler only had centimetres on it. One inch equalled about two and a half centimetres. Mory counted along her ruler. Two and a half equals one. Five equals two. Ten equals four. Twenty equals eight. Thirty equals twelve. And twelve inches equals one foot. She took a piece of baler twine from her pocket and measured out thirty centimetres once then twice and cut it.

"That is two feet," she informed Splodge. In acknowledgement he stretched a paw across the duvet where he lay curled and contented.

Mory hung the twine against the table leg. It nearly reached the top.

"Hell's bells," she said. "That's high." She imagined all the jumps as high as her table and that they would look like her table. The whole course stretched into a series of tables. She tried turning the tables into poles like proper jumps but the tables stayed and seemed big and cumbersome and frightening. She stared glumly at the entry form wondering if she would dare to jump after all.

Peering round the door Cara found Mory, slumped, chin in hands, still staring.

"Hey, what's up?"

"I've just worked out how big two feet is. All the jumps in the novice class will be this high." Mory stretched the baler twine against the table leg.

"You've jumped that high on Misty and thought nothing of it."

"Have I?"

"Anyway not all the jumps will be that high, some will be smaller."

"I hope so."

"Why worry? Dancer can jump that easily. Remember what Mrs Ashfield said about her jumping as high as a five-bar gate? Well, the field gate comes up to here on me." Cara held her hand at shoulder height.

"But I fell off."

"Only because you weren't expecting it."

"You're right," Mory said. "I was having a fit of the glums." Cara raised her eyebrows and Mory laughed. "It's what Mum says. Anyway, what can I do for you?"

"You're not going to like this," said Cara. "It's all Mum's fault. You know she was talking to Mr Spencer …"

"Yes," said Mory, expecting something unpleasant.

"Well, he was saying that Caroline didn't have anyone to ride with and nowhere to go which wasn't on the road so Mum said he could bring Caroline and Doughnut over any time and she could ride here."

"Oh, no!"

"She's coming tomorrow afternoon. But don't worry. It's not you Mum's volunteered. It's me. I've got to take her for a nice hack on the hills. This is to warn you the Spencer's on her way."

"I'm surprised she wants to come."

"Maybe she doesn't. Maybe her dad's making her like my mum's making me."

"Aren't parents awful," said Mory. Being dragged off to buy the trainers had been bad enough. "Look, I would come with you but …" Mory knew she would be with Lionel and felt guilty for not saying so. It was the first secret she'd kept from Cara.

"Don't worry. Josh might come. Anyway, it's probably better if I take her on my own. There'll be less arguments."

"True," said Mory. Then dismissing it she turned back to the entry form. "I'm going to fill this in."

"Great, I'll help you. And I'll do mine." Cara pulled a crumpled piece of paper from her pocket and perched on the end of the bed. "You know, you're going to be fine."

Mory chewed the end of her pen. If I'm going to be fine I must jump the fallen oak, she thought. It seemed the only way to success. She filled in her name at the top of the entry form and under the Class column wrote, One Novice Jumping, and under Name of Pony, Midnight Dancer.

# SEVEN

# *Dead Find*

Sunday morning was *hard labour in the pottery*. That's what David called it but Mory thought it fun to put up shelves on the painted white wall. Here pots would dry out or wait to be glazed. In the cowshed finished pots would sit in neat, shiny rows.

"Hold this a sec," said David, lining up a bracket over the holes he had drilled and plugged. "I'll get a screwdriver." It didn't take a moment to screw up. "Do you think you could do that?"

"Sure," said Mory.

"Off you go then. You can put up the bottom brackets." Mory found that turning the screwdriver *was* hard work after all. She watched David begin on the higher brackets.

"I can't get the screws right in like you do."

"Don't worry," said David, "I'll tighten them later. Just getting the brackets in position is a help." Mory did her best, aided by strenuous grunts. Soon her wrist ached and the red patch on her palm felt like the beginnings of a blister.

"Heck, Dad, why don't you get one of those electric screwdrivers?"

"I know! I said it was hard labour but once they're up, they're up."

Mory knelt back and took a breather. Her mind wandered to the entry form waiting on her table. Each class cost one pound fifty to enter. Besides the Novice Jumping, she was going to do the Pony Club dressage test, the Handy Pony competition and the flag race. They needed a team of four for that. Cara, Josh, herself and Lionel if he would. With four different competitions, one of them jumping, she expected it to be the most exciting day of her life.

"What's happened to my helper?" smiled David. "Had enough?"

"Wrist ache but I'll finish."

Mory picked up the screwdriver and worked with renewed vigour, finishing at last hot and red-faced.

"Done it," she said looking at the line of brackets with satisfaction.

Sheila poked her head round the door.

"Mory, collect the eggs for me, will you? Josh has forgotten! I'm in the middle of baking and I've run out."

"Typical," said Mory. She knew Josh was up at Llangabby. He'd rushed off after breakfast.

On her way to the porch for egg boxes she met Cara.

"I'm taking Misty up to Llangabby. I've got to get

ready for the ride with Caroline," she said. "Do you want to do jumping practice later?"

"Tomorrow, after school," said Mory.

"Why not today?"

"I've got too much to do," said Mory vaguely. Her secret rendezvous with Lionel weighed heavily. But later she planned to set up a jumping course in the Llangabby paddock, along with a handy pony course if she could think of enough obstacles, ready for tomorrow.

"I'm coming up after I've done the eggs," Mory said.

"I'll wait for you."

"I'll bring Misty's tack if you like."

"Thanks," said Cara. "It'll save me coming back for it."

Most of the hens were in the run outside the hen house, clucking and pecking, ruffled brown, seeking worms hither and thither on their scaly yellow legs. With care Mory lifted each nesting box lid in case a hen was laying. Mory envied Josh this job. Finding an egg was like finding treasure. She found eight, all speckled brown, one of them still warm. She carried them to the house, marvelling that the hens didn't protest at such thieving, and knowing that tomorrow there would be more.

Cara had brought Misty in and was waiting in the yard. Mory took the eggs indoors. Hurrying out again she looked in the paddock. Rustler and Dancer were grazing side by side. Mory felt a thrill of anticipation at the thought of what she and Dancer were going to do later.

After collecting Misty's tack the two girls and the pony set off up the track. Seeing but not seeing, Mory kicked at a granite chip. Caroline Spencer had crept back into her thoughts again. How she wished she wouldn't.

"I wish Mum wouldn't organize things for me," sighed Cara, also pensive. "It really is a drag having to ride with Caroline. Of course, I do feel sorry for her being on her own and all that but ..." She trailed off.

"You're much nicer than me," said Mory. "I would have refused."

"It's different though, isn't it? Caroline's not always getting at me for a start. And she's never had anything to do with Misty. I'd feel differently if he'd been hers even if it was just for twenty-four hours."

"Poor Dancer," said Mory, remembering. "Just think what Caroline might have done to her!" They continued in silence.

"She seems to be getting on all right with Doughnut," Cara said at last. "That's a good thing."

"I suppose," said Mory who felt sorry for Doughnut. Lucky she was a tolerant pony. Caroline got cross with her at the drop of a hat. "She always blames Doughnut if anything goes wrong. She never thinks it might be her."

"She must know really. Look how Lionel shows her

up by riding Tawney so well. No wonder she doesn't want him any more."

"Lionel says everyone falls off," said Mory, thinking of her own tumbles as well as Caroline's.

"They do," said Cara.

"You've not fallen off once since I've known you."

"Ah, but I have lots of times in the past. Just not recently, touch wood." Cara patted her head several times. "I prefer not to," she said laughing.

"I know how you feel," said Mory shifting the saddle further up her arm. They walked the rest of the way in thoughtful silence.

A protest of bleating met them at the top of the track. The yard gate was closed against a flock of milling sheep indignant at being herded from their field.

"They're going through the footbath," said Cara. "I forgot. I suppose I'll have to wait." Misty gave Cara a nudge as if to say, if we're waiting how about a snack? Cara gave him an affectionate rub. "Stop it," she said.

"I'll put the tack in the tack room," said Mory, leaning the saddle on the gate so she could climb over. Then she waded through the swirling sheep.

"Mind you don't get knocked over," shouted Uncle Glyn from the other side of the yard.

"I will," called Mory, chub chub chubbing at the sheep to make a pathway for herself.

"Okay Josh, lift the gate," said Uncle Glyn. "Back Mab."

The baaing rose to a crescendo as sheep were sent

one at a time along an alleyway to the footbath. Quite a traffic jam, thought Mory, watching the first go through. Mab circled behind, making sure none turned away. Mory popped the tack in the tack room and strolled to the barn. Some minutes later Josh found her cuddling a roly-poly black and white puppy.

"Will Mab mind?" she asked.

"She doesn't mind me. Which one have you got?" Mory uncurled her hands. "No that's not mine," said Josh. Mab appeared in the doorway and cocked her head to one side before trotting over, her work done, to lie down amongst her brood. "Good girl, Mab," said Josh, stroking her. Her arrival excited a burst of activity amongst her babies. The pup in Mory's hands whined and wriggled until put down near her mother where she joined in the competition for a drink.

"Aren't they lovely," said Mory, "and haven't they grown already?" She stroked Mab's silky back. "Which one is yours?"

"Mine is …" Josh tried to see amongst the pile of little bottoms, "… this one, I think. She's got a white tip to her tail and a white patch over one eye."

"Oh yes," said Mory. "I can see her. What a pudding." Mory laughed. "But then they're all puddings. Have you thought of a name?"

"Little Nipper, Nip for short because she does," said Josh

"Nip," echoed Mory. "Yes, that's nice. Which is the other girl?"

"She's not so easy to find when they're in a scrum like this. I think it's this one." Josh stroked a wriggling back but it did not distract her. "She's very determined as you can see."

"Are their personalities coming out already?"

"I like to think so," said Josh. "But it's hard to tell really."

"They're adorable," sighed Mory.

There was a call from the barn door. A summons to come and eat. Reluctantly they left Mab to her puppies and went indoors.

As it happened it was Mory who opened the gate for the Spencers. She was on her way to Black Rock when their car and trailer arrived. They had all come. Mr and Mrs Spencer in the front, Caroline pouting in the back. The others were still indoors and, in order to be helpful, Mory fetched them.

"Are you going on this ride?" she asked Josh. He screwed up his face.

"Don't think so. I'm helping put the sheep back." Rows of silent, furry faces stared at them from the bottom yard.

"Neither am I. I feel mean leaving it to Cara, but I'd only get into a row if I went."

"That's hard to believe," said Josh, widening his eyes in pretend astonishment. Mory aimed a dig.

When Cara and Aunt Olwen came out to greet their guests Mory whispered "Good luck," in Cara's ear before slipping out of the gate. Once on the track she ran, her legs gathering momentum with the steepness of the hill. She arrived in the Black Rock yard with triumphant speed and stopped at the paddock gate. Dancer and Rustler ignored her and carried on eating. Mory draped herself across the gate until she got her breath back.

"Right, Dancer, now for some fun!" she said and went to fetch a halter.

Trotting up the sheep track to the ridge was as exhilarating as ever. There was something about the blue sky, the mew of a buzzard and Dancer's eagerness. At such moments Mory ached with love for her black pony. She let the reins go, stood in the stirrups and flung her arms around Dancer's neck. Given such freedom Dancer broke into a canter and, laughing, Mory quickly gathered up the reins and brought Dancer back to a trot.

"You wickedness," she said, stroking the pony's neck. "You'd go galloping off if I let you."

They cantered along the ridge to the rock crop where Mory slowed to a walk. She scanned the moorland ahead, hoping to see Lionel. Some distant sheep took flight but Mory could see no reason for it as they bobbed and weaved out of view. She trotted on, taking the sheep path down to the fallen oak, keeping Old Mr Lewis's cottage, or rather Hill Farm, as she tried to think of it now, in her sights. Smoke curled from the chimney but there was no sign of the green Range Rover or the grey dog Hector.

"Just as well," she told Dancer, "or you wouldn't be behaving yourself."

Lionel was sitting on the oak, heels braced against the bark, whittling at a stick. He looked up and grinned.

"Saw you come off the ridge," he said. "Looking good."

"She's full of go," said Mory, eyeing the fallen oak. It looked big. Lionel slid to the ground.

"It's not that big," he said as if he knew what Mory was thinking. "Do you want me to take her over first?" Mory was startled. She hadn't thought that Lionel might want to ride Dancer.

"I …"

"There's no need," he said. "You can do it. Now watch." Lionel paced a large circle from the fallen trunk round the gaping roots and the large hole they had left back to the tree. "See that circle? Canter that on the right rein. Let her take the tree-trunk in her stride. If you come round on that circle she'll be right." Lionel seemed confident.

It was more than Mory felt but she took her courage in her hands and trotted round the top of the fallen oak. She turned onto the circle and asked for a canter. Right leg leading on a right-hand circle.

"Great," said Lionel. "Off you go." Round they came and there was the tree. Dancer's ears pricked.

One, two, three and into the air. They soared above the trunk and were over it before Mory could catch her breath. "Go on round and do it again," came the command. "Keep her collected. Meet it like that again. It was dead right."

This time Mory could see the strides. They met it perfectly and Dancer leapt the tree as if it was nothing.

"Round again," said Lionel. "Shorten her up a bit." Yes, Mory could see she needed a smaller stride to take her into two bigger ones to get to the right take off place. "Fantastic," cried a delighted Lionel, pink with pleasure at his pupil's success. "You put her right there. One more time." This time Dancer met it just right and Mory let her take it in her stride. "See, she's not jumping it so big now. She's getting the hang of it." Both pony and rider were more sure of themselves.

"Well done, Dancer, well done," said Mory stroking the pony's neck.

"Give her a break and then do it on the other rein," said Lionel. "She's a cracker, isn't she? Getting it sussed nicely."

Mory walked Dancer round for a few minutes and then turned and trotted round the other way. She came in on the left-hand circle.

"Heck Lionel, it's downhill this way."

"Just hold her together and don't let her run away with you. She's nimble. Trust her. She won't let you down."

It was true. Mory came round, saw three strides in, leant into the jump, sat up and kept turning whilst pushing the pony into her hands.

"And again," came the command. Lionel's face had a cheeky, pleased look as he watched Mory steady the pony, find the stride and jump.

"Wicked," he cried. "Just wicked."

Dancer came round for the third time as eager as if it was the first. She cleared the tree like a bird skimming water. Mory slowed, patting and praising, delighted with herself and the pony.

"We did it," she puffed. "We did it."

"Well done, young lady, well done." The voice was so unexpected that Mory jumped. Dancer stiffened. Watching above them was the lady and the dog.

"Better than last time, eh?" As they approached Dancer tried to whip round but Mory held her and made her face them, talking soothingly all the time.

"Whoa, pony, whoa, girl. It's all right."

"Don't let her turn," encouraged Lionel. "Steady girl." And he joined in to soothe, bringing pony nuts from his pocket. Cautiously Dancer took them, with an eye firmly on the dog. But when he did nothing, just stayed by his mistress, she relaxed a little. Lionel kept his arm over Dancer's neck, nuzzling her coat with his fingers.

"I hope you don't mind us being here," said Mory. "It's just that I wanted to jump the tree properly."

"And so you did," said the lady. "Hector and I heard hoofbeats and came to investigate. That's all.

Goodbye." She turned and the dog went with her back up the slope towards Hill Farm.

"Phew," said Mory. "I thought she was going to tell us off. She must have come back while we were jumping."

"Some dog," said Lionel. "Big. Like you said. Could be Ben's dad to look at him."

"I think we'd better go," said Mory. "Come back for tea?"

"Okay."

"Thanks Lionel. You really helped." Lionel went pink and silent. "Would you like a ride on Dancer?" He shook his head.

"You ride her well," he said. "You go together. That's a fact." It was Mory's turn to go pink, which she did, with pleasure.

Mory climbed the sheep track and Lionel picked a pathway, wandering in and out amongst the heather.

"Did you come on your bike?" Mory asked.

"It's by the cattle grid," he replied, then tripped, landing on his knees with a grunt.

"Lionel!" cried Mory slipping from Dancer. "Are you all right?"

"Yes," said Lionel. "I'm fine but this ain't." He prodded a bundle of wool and his finger met still flesh. A feeling of dread gripped Mory.

"It's not …" Lionel nodded.

"Dead sheep," he muttered. He lifted back its head. The throat was a mass of congealed blood. Life had been ripped from it. "Dog!"

"How horrible," said Mory shuddering. Dancer snorted beside her. "Lionel, it wasn't …"

"No, it wasn't Ben." His eyes met hers. "I swear it." Then with one accord they looked towards Hill Farm, both wondering.

"I'd better tell Uncle Glyn," said Mory.

"You must," Lionel said.

# EIGHT

## *Runaway*

They found Uncle Glyn in the lower barn checking his cows. Most had already calved; a few were still due. Mory led Dancer closer. She hated bringing bad news. Lionel trailed behind, unsure.

"Uncle Glyn!"

He turned and met a grave face.

"What's up?" he asked.

"We found a dead sheep. Up on the hills."

"Whereabouts?" He stared at the two anxious faces. "Are you sure it was dead?"

"Lionel fell over it."

"It's dead," said Lionel, knowing full well the news meant loss.

"And?" said Uncle Glyn.

"A dog had it."

"Hell!" said Uncle Glyn and stormed up the yard. "Put that pony in a stable," he shouted. "You'll have to show me where it is." Mory looked helplessly at Lionel.

"Better do as he says."

Mory led Dancer to Misty's stable and untacked

her while Lionel fetched a flap of hay. Mory checked the water bucket and gave Dancer all the pony nuts in her pocket. Dancer nuzzled her for more, tickling Mory's hands with insistent lips.

"All gone," said Mory. "We won't be long." She was sad. Sad for the dead sheep and sad for the dog that had savaged it. If Uncle Glyn caught the dog it too would die. She stroked Dancer's soft muzzle. It was a blight over their great jumping achievement.

"It's horrible," she said. "I don't want anything else to die."

"Hurry up, Mory," said Uncle Glyn. "Are you coming Lionel?" Lionel hesitated, then seeing Mory's miserable expression nodded. Both youngsters climbed into the Landrover.

Uncle Glyn started the engine and swung the vehicle round. His face was livid red and Mory knew he was very, very angry.

Just like the other day, she thought. She caught Lionel's eye and grimaced. Without expression, Lionel turned away. She felt alone, locked between her raging uncle and the distant boy, and all she could do was hold tight as the Landrover bumped and lurched and wish she didn't have to go back.

"Where is it?" said Uncle Glyn. They had reached the rock crop.

"Down there," said Mory pointing. Uncle Glyn stopped and they climbed out. She and Lionel had to run to keep up.

"Where?"

"It was here, wasn't it?" She was confused. Lionel bent down and picked up some tufts of wool. There were dark specks in it.

"Dried blood," he said. "It *was* here but it's gone." Uncle Glyn took the wool. He muttered something under his breath and swung round, his gaze settling on Hill Farm. Then he stormed back towards the ridge. Mory and Lionel scrambled after him.

"What do you think he's going to do?" Mory panted.

"Dunno," said Lionel. "He's really mad."

"There's not much he can do, is there, if he hasn't got the corpse?"

"He's angry enough to do anything," said Lionel.

They clambered back into the Landrover. Fortunately, Uncle Glyn didn't do what Mory dreaded, which was drive to Hill Farm. Instead he swung round and headed for home. What a relief! Tears pricked Mory's eyes. Poor dead sheep! She sniffed.

"It's all right," said Uncle Glyn. "Don't let it worry you now. Things die. Get killed. It happens."

It did worry Mory. The only other dead thing she had ever seen was Fluff, her guinea pig, and she had cried for days over him. She had made him a grave and everything. Marked it with a little cross and put flowers there. Who was going to do that for the sheep?

"Once you're dead, you're dead," said Lionel

shrugging. Death didn't seem to bother him. Not in the same way. Mory knew he'd seen other dead creatures, maybe even killed them. She thought about Lionel's dad, Mr Jones and his chickens. Chickens sold to eat as well as to lay eggs. Had Lionel wrung a hen's neck? An image of protesting, flapping wings flashed into her mind followed by the limpness of death. Her hands covered her face and she sobbed.

"Now, now, lovely," said Uncle Glyn taking a hand off the steering wheel and putting his arm round her. "I don't like to see them dead either."

Lionel sat uncomfortably. Death was death. Like Mr Morgan said, it happened. It wasn't nice but it was only a sheep. If it wasn't dead now it would be later. That's what sheep were bred for, to go to the butcher's and be eaten. It wasn't a nice death but the dog killed it quick. He thought of Ben. Whose dog had done it? That was the puzzler. Well it wasn't his. Ben was tied up safe at Penyworlod and it was a relief to know it.

The Landrover set the cattle grid ringing before they turned into the Llangabby yard. Mr and Mrs Spencer were back with car and trailer. So were Cara and Caroline. The ponies stood sweaty and patient while the girls ran up stirrups and loosened off their girths, chatting about their ride until the Landrover interrupted them and Cara waved. Mory dredged some tissue segments from a pocket, wiped her eyes and blew her nose.

"Better?" inquired Uncle Glyn. She nodded. She did not want Caroline to see her crying.

Uncle Glyn drove slowly through the yard and parked by the bottom barn out of the way. It gave Mory a chance to recover. By the time the three of them walked up to the yard she was composed.

"That's my girl," said Uncle Glyn patting her shoulder. "I'll sort it out, don't you worry." Uncle Glyn crossed to the Spencers, amiable, friendly, as if nothing had happened. Lionel made for his bike.

"What about tea, Lionel?" Mory asked. He shook his head.

"No, ta. Better get going." Yes, because of Caroline. Mory knew that. She sighed and drew closer.

"Thanks, Lionel. Thanks for everything." Whispered words. Caroline was craning to hear. "See you at school tomorrow."

Lionel swung himself astride his bike.

"You and Dancer got to show her, see. And you can." Lionel pedalled to the gate. He was met by a bundle of grey fur, ecstatic with joy, which almost knocked him flying. Ben had found what he was looking for. He whimpered and licked the embarrassed boy, trailing the baler twine lead that should have had him tied safely at Penyworlod.

"What you doing here?" said Lionel.

"Yes, what is he doing here?" said Caroline, her strident tone drawing everyone's attention. "I didn't think dogs were allowed to run wild on farms. It's

dangerous for the sheep isn't it?"

Mory glared an unmistakable look. Even Caroline was affected. "Well, it is, isn't it?" She looked round for support.

Uncle Glyn eyed Ben.

"Is this yours?" he asked.

"Yes, don't tell Dad, will you? Please, don't tell him, Mr Morgan."

"Why not? Chases sheep does he?"

"No," said Lionel. "No. Dad don't know I got him." He blushed red to match the colour of his hair. "He got loose. How he knew I was here I don't know."

"It's Ben," said Mory. "He lives at Penyworld. Megan and Ian know all about him." She was desperate to make it all right.

"What a nice surprise," said Cara backing Mory up. "How clever of him to find you."

Uncle Glyn took a few swift steps and grabbed Ben by the scruff of the neck. He inspected the surprised dog's face, teeth and paws, looking for wool, dried blood, any clue that might give the dog away.

"It wasn't him," said Lionel. "I left him tied at Penyworlod. He can't have been loose long."

Uncle Glyn stood up and let the dog go. Ben cowered against Lionel's legs, upset by the roughness.

"I'm training him to work sheep," said Lionel.

"Him?" said Uncle Glyn.

"He can do it."

"I'm warning you, Lionel, if I catch him loose on my land or up on the hills I'll let him have it. I'm taking no chances. Not after today. I'm going to get to the bottom of it. It could have been him I saw the other day." Lionel lowered his head, a hand on Ben, comforting him, knowing that his one playful gambol after a sheep might cost him his life.

"Uncle Glyn, please," said Mory.

"There's no room for sentiment in farming, Mory. I can't afford any more losses and I'm going to make sure I don't get any."

"But Ben wouldn't kill a sheep. Lionel's training him."

"Not with my sheep he doesn't. You've heard what I said, Lionel, and I mean it."

Lionel didn't doubt it. Wounded and bleak he

picked up the trailing baler twine lead and, pulling his dog and pushing his bike, went out of the gate. It wasn't until he was out of sight that he let Ben go and pedalled hard for Penyworlod, with the dog running at his side.

"Well," said Uncle Glyn rubbing his hands together, conscious of everyone staring. "Let's hope I've sorted that one out." Cara knew well enough not to ask questions. It was Josh who did, arriving at this moment on Rustler.

"What's going on?" His voice rang loud and clear.

"Nothing," said Mory through clenched teeth, and hurried to the tack room where she kicked the feed bin hard, twice. It was her turn to be very, very angry.

Next morning in the playground, Mory waited until the last minute for Lionel and Ben but they didn't arrive. She dragged her feet to the door, still hoping they were coming but there was no sign of them.

"Come on in, Mory. What are you doing dithering outside?" said Mrs Price.

Pulling off her anorak Mory went to the cloakroom. She flung her bag on the bench and tripped over someone's foot.

"Ouch!"

"Sorry."

"Look where you're going, you!" And the foot kicked out at her. She dodged it. Its owner stood up, brimming with indignation. As soon as Mory saw it was Caroline she walked off. It had taken her a while to realize that the one thing Caroline hated was to be ignored.

In the classroom Mory hung her bag over her chair and slumped down next to Cara.

"He's not here then?" her cousin asked. Mory shook her head. "He's probably just late."

"I hope that's all," said Mory.

"If he does turn up I've got some sandwiches for Ben."

"That's nice of you." She hadn't really talked much to Cara since Uncle Glyn had sent Lionel off with a flea in his ear. His words. She heard him say that to the Spencers. Did Uncle Glyn really believe that Ben had killed his sheep? Mory didn't. But if it wasn't Ben and it wasn't Mrs Ashfield's dog, whose dog was it?

"Mory! Mory Harper!" Mory came to with a start. "Yes, Mrs Wynne."

"Come here a minute will you?" Mory got up and squeezed round the end of the table. Caroline put out her foot. Mory saw it and banged into it. Serve her right.

"Sorry," said Mory, meaning, I hope that hurt. Caroline rubbed the banged place but said nothing. There was not much she could say when she had meant Mory to fall over.

"I saw that," whispered Josh from his table.

"She's a pig!" Mory whispered back. She arrived at Mrs Wynne's table and stood patiently.

"This was in the school letter box. Well, take it. It's addressed to you."

Mory took the grubby brown envelope. On it was written MORY HARPER in big scrawling letters. She knew instantly who it was from and wanted to hide the envelope from the many eyes gazing inquisitively at it. She crumpled it as though it was nothing and shoved it in her pocket, making her way quickly to her place. She sat down, opened her notebook and started to write. Everyone was looking at her. Her heart beat madly. Behave normally. It she didn't she might give something away.

For most people the envelope soon ceased to be of interest. It was obvious she wasn't going to open it. She caught Cara's eye but couldn't say anything. Caroline still had her under scrutiny. She pretended it was perfectly normal to be given a letter by her teacher at the beginning of the school day. At the first opportunity to be private she would open it. She was longing to know what it said.

At breaktime she made her way to the girls' toilet as fast as she was able without arousing suspicion. Locked behind the door she pulled the envelope from her pocket. Feeling like secret agent Harper she read,

I'm bunking off a bit. Meet me Monday after school, half past five. Go past H. F. Take sheep track what

goes straight up. Follow to trees and stream. I got something to ask. Important. DO NOT TELL.
LJ

So that was it. Lionel Jones had run away. He's done it to save Ben, she thought, and she admired him for it.

DO NOT TELL. That made it awkward. She wanted to tell Cara and Josh. She wanted them to know how brave Lionel was to go into the hills by himself. Never mind. She would meet him and take him some supplies. It was the least she could do.

Carefully she folded the letter and put it back in her pocket. Then, as a secret agent would, she flushed the toilet, even though she hadn't used it, before letting herself out. She wandered into the playground pretending to have not a care in the world while secretly she planned her meeting, hoping that nothing would get in the way.

# NINE

## *Rendezvous*

Mory fielded questions about her letter by saying it was from an old friend. She was truthful with Cara but would say no more than that it was from Lionel. Mory longed to confide in her and spent an uncomfortable day trying to reconcile her conflicting loyalties. She wanted to share Lionel's daring but could not think how to do it without betraying him.

Going home on the bus the two girls sat in silence. Josh was, as usual, with his friends at the back. Cara broke the awkwardness.

"What time shall we start jumping practice?" she asked. Mory had forgotten all about it. Her only thoughts were about supplies for Lionel and involved baked beans and tin-openers and what would fit in her rucksack.

"Oh, er … can we do it tomorrow?"

"You put it off yesterday and now you're putting it off today."

Heck, thought Mory, and I still haven't told Cara about jumping the oak tree. Guilt made her defensive.

"I know, I know, it's just that I've got something really important to do," she snapped.

"What's more important than practising for the Penyworld show?" Cara was surprisingly fierce.

"Nothing," said Mory, "only what I've got to do can't wait."

"Is it for Uncle David?"

"Not exactly." Mory remembered the birthday mural. "But I have got to plan his birthday present."

"Can I help?"

"Not really." Mory squirmed inside. "Thanks. I need to do it on my own."

"You said you wanted to do well on Dancer."

"I do. I'll practise tomorrow and all the other days but I can't tonight."

Cara let out a big sigh and stared out of the window.

"Josh and I will just have to practise on our own then." Another big sigh.

"I'm sorry," said Mory. "You must think I'm a real heel."

"What I think doesn't count."

Mory couldn't see how to make it any better so she left it. When the bus pulled up at their lay-by she got off first and, leaving Cara and Josh to make their way together, hurried on ahead.

Changed and ready Mory rummaged in the kitchen for things to take. Matches, baked beans, the camping tin-opener, teabags, a cola bottle with some milk, a polythene bag with a few slices of bread. A tin of Splodge's cat food for Ben. She noted down what she needed to replace and stuffed her rucksack. She'd go to the shop in Llantrist. Mrs Pugh had most things. She'd ask to go at lunchtime or try and make it after school before the bus left. Thank goodness she had lots of money. She thought wistfully of riding gear but wasn't going to let Lionel down.

It was lucky that yesterday the ponies had been moved up to Llangabby. She gave Splodge his tea and swung her rucksack over her shoulder. Fortunately Sheila wasn't back yet. She let herself out of the front door to avoid the yard and any awkward questions David might ask. She had told enough lies and half-truths already.

Mory trudged up the track. The weight on her back was surprisingly heavy and she hoped it wouldn't unbalance her when riding. She dreaded meeting her mum, expecting her to drive down at any minute. Luck was with her. She reached the lane without that happening and veered off to the cattle grid. She left the rucksack behind some rocks and went to get Dancer ready.

The yard was empty. Mory guessed Cara and Josh were indoors having tea. She wondered if Aunt Olwen would miss her. She fetched Dancer from the field, tied her up and ran a brush over the bits that mattered. It felt wrong not grooming her properly. She picked out her feet and, with a speed that surprised the pony, tacked her up. She tied Dancer's headcollar and rope round her waist and hurried them both out of the yard.

Just in time. Going through the cattle grid gate she heard a car in the lane. A hasty shove sent the gate home and the latch clicked. Grabbing her rucksack, she ran. Dancer, unused to such rude behaviour, pulled back at first before trotting obligingly alongside.

"Good pony, good girl," said Mory. "I don't think she saw. Sorry to rush you." When they were out of sight Dancer received a stroke of appreciation. Mory pulled on the rucksack and tightened the girth. Pulling down the stirrups she mounted. Settled in the saddle she took a quick look at her watch.

"Let's go," she said. Familiar words to the pony who flicked her ears back and jogged, anticipating a gallop. "Now, now, now," said Mory. "There's no need to go mad." She insisted on a walk while she got used to the weight on her back.

"Saddlebags are what I need," she mused. "One day."

They began to trot. As ever Mory was enjoying her ride and the different route to the rock crop. She asked for a canter, nice and collected, no rushing. The bag banged. It was not comfortable and, as she reached over her shoulder to adjust it, a large white van rushed at them from behind the rocks. Dancer jumped sharply sideways to avoid it. Mory glimpsed the driver's alarmed face as he swerved and stopped.

"You all right?" he shouted through the open window.

"Yes, thanks," said Mory, shaken. Dancer seemed surprisingly unconcerned.

"Sorry about that." And with a wave the man drove on. GRIFFITHS FOR PLUMBING stared at them from the back doors. Mory guessed he must have come from Hill Farm.

"Phew," she said. "That could have been nasty."

Riding from the rock crop Mory could see smoke rising from Mrs Ashfield's chimney and it wasn't long before she saw the Range Rover parked in its usual place. She took out Lionel's note. *Go past HF. Take sheep track which goes straight up. Follow to trees and stream.* Not brilliant directions but HF was obviously Hill Farm. Mory didn't want to go too close. She turned away from the main track to the south intending to loop round to the sheep track on the other side of the dip. That must be the path Lionel wanted her to take. Then once on the next ridge she guessed it would be downhill to the trees and the stream.

Away from the main track the going was rough. Sometimes a sheep path went in the direction they wanted, otherwise they crossed heather and tufted grass. They skirted a patch of sodden peat with bog grasses growing spiky and dark and came closer to Hill Farm than Mory meant. But the house seemed quiet and she was sure she hadn't been seen.

Turning away, she climbed to the ridge, joining a sheep track near the top.

"This must be right," she said, pleased.

Mory followed the path down from the ridge and soon even the drifting chimney smoke was out of sight. Ahead the path led into a steep-sided gully where weathered rock gave way to patches of grass high above. Several sheep grazed there, looking down at her as she rode by. Dancer blew through her nostrils. The burbling sound startled the two nearest sheep. They scampered away before turning to stare. Mory laughed.

"Did you do that on purpose?" she asked.

They walked on down the narrow gully until it opened out. The land, stretching rock-strewn before them, was a valley where the music of running water enticed them forward and a buzzard mew was tossed from rock to rock in eerie echo. Mory searched for the bird until she saw it wheeling against the grey sky. The plaintive call came again. It was a lonely place.

Ahead were the trees and Mory was glad to see them. As the path evened out she let Dancer trot, her hoof beats ringing out against clipped stone. They stopped by the trees. They grew tall as willowy sentinels and between them flowed the stream. Mory looked at her watch. A quarter past five. She was early. She let Dancer amble towards the water in case she was thirsty. The pony blew and pawed making wonderful splashes.

"No, no, no," said Mory. "It's to drink." But Dancer wouldn't drink.

Mory waited It was the waiting that unsettled her. She kept looking round but there was no sight of Lionel. When she did see him she nearly jumped out of her skin.

"Where did you come from?" she gasped. He grinned up at her. At his side Ben grinned too, mouth open, tongue lolling.

"Followed you from Hill Farm."

"I never saw you."

"You weren't s'posed to." Lionel gently pulled one of Ben's ears. "I wanted to be sure you got here."

"And I did," said Mory, dismounting and dropping her rucksack to the ground. "I've brought some supplies. How come I didn't spot you?"

"I was careful. An' I weren't always behind you. An' I ducked a lot. Good practice." He grinned. "That's what I was gonna ask. For supplies. I gotta den. Wanna see?"

"Okay."

Mory ran up her stirrups, tucked the reins behind them and loosened Dancer's girth. She untied the headcollar from her waist and put it on, clipping on the lead rope. Mory offered a handful of pony nuts, which were gratefully received, and looked round for a tying place.

"Over here," said Lionel. A piece of baler twine was secured ready round a sturdy sapling. "She'll be fine tied to that." Ben was lapping a long, cool drink from the stream. "Is she thirsty?"

"I offered her a drink when we got here," Mory said.

"Are you? The water's fresh."

"That reminds me. I've got teabags and milk. Baked beans and bread. Matches and cat food. I didn't think Ben would mind that."

"I got no tin-opener."

"Yes, you have," said Mory producing it in triumph.

"Great," said Lionel. "I didn't think much about food. I'm relying on him. He got us a rabbit. Want some? There's a bit left." Mory shook her head. Lionel laughed. "You eat chicken. What's wrong with rabbit?" Mory pulled a face. She didn't know but something was.

"Did you cook it?"

"'Course I did. On sticks. Works a treat."

"Show us your den."

"Can't you see it?" Mory looked round. She saw Ben by the stream. Dancer resigned to a wait beginning to doze. Trees, bushes, scrub, rocks. Nowhere was anything that looked like a den.

"Is it a cave?"

"Follow me," said Lionel, pleased as anything. "I've been working on it all day." He lead the way to some bushes growing between two stout saplings. It was when they got close that Mory saw the bushes were camouflage, laced skilfully together over what seemed like a tarpaulin suspended between the saplings by a rope.

"Lionel, that's brilliant!"

Lionel bent down and wriggled under the bushes, disappearing inside. Mory bent down and did the same. It was dark inside and smelt of damp ground. Slowly her eyes adjusted.

"There's nothing on the floor," she said. "What happens if it rains?"

"The tarp'll keep it out. Most of it."

There was rustling and Ben wriggled his way in, tail wagging, giving wet doggy kisses to one then the other and back again.

"Gerroff," said Lionel.

"Stop it," said Mory, burying her head in her arms and curling up. "Get him off." She giggled and spluttered until Ben stopped.

"He likes you," said Lionel.

"I like him," said Mory, stroking Ben's soft furry head, feeling his trust.

Suddenly Ben stiffened and a low rumble came from his throat.

"Something's out there," whispered Lionel and put a finger to his lips. Mory's face creased with anxiety.

"Dancer," she whispered. Lionel nodded. Snake-like he wriggled soundlessly outside. The rumble in Ben's throat grew louder and he rushed after Lionel.

There was horrible snarling and Mory, anxious for her pony, scrambled out as fast as she could. Two dogs and two owners faced each other across the clearing. Lionel held Ben and Mrs Ashfield, upright and stern, Hector. Dancer, four square and alert, was ready to bolt. She had only to pull back and the baler twine would snap.

"And what have I found? A pair of runaways?"

"Please," said Mory. "Please, don't let them fight. They're frightening my pony."

# TEN

# *Mrs Ashfield*

Mrs Ashfield was perfectly calm.

"Go to your pony," she told Mory keeping her eyes on the unkempt boy and the dog. What were they doing now, these children? she wondered.

Mory approached Dancer, talking gently. She struggled with the quick release knot, moving with Dancer as she backed, hand on the bridle, knowing that if the pony whipped round and bolted she'd have to let go. She stroked Dancer's neck then distracted her by pushing her shoulder to back her away from the two snarling dogs.

With distance between her and her terror Dancer became more manageable and allowed Mory to lead her away. When it was safe Mory tightened the girth and took off the headcollar. She was up in a moment feeling more in control mounted than on the ground. She turned to go back.

Approaching the den Mory was surprised and pleased to see the two dogs sniffing and marking out their territory in a friendly, dog-like way. There was no sign of a fight. Mrs Ashfield was talking to Lionel. It was a serious conversation from the look of Lionel's drooping head and embarrassed scuffling. Dancer came to an abrupt stop when she saw Hector.

"Go on," said Mory sternly, urging her forward with drumming heels. "Get on with you." Turning Dancer's head this way then that, giving her no chance to whip round. Mory's shouting startled a ewe who ran straight for the dogs, her twin lambs following.

"Down!" came the double command, the woman's and the boy's. Both dogs went down and the ewe nearly ran between them before she realized what they were.

"Ben, go away," cried Lionel and the dog was up. Two sharp whistles followed and the dog was behind the ewe. "Down." Down he went. Another whistle and he was up again, sending ewe and lambs back the way they had come. "Ben, come away." And back to Lionel to sit at heel. The sheep bobbed past.

Mory wished Uncle Glyn could have seen. Lionel had trained the dog well. She urged Dancer on. "Hector isn't going to hurt you." Reluctantly Dancer went.

"Let's get her used to him," said Mrs Ashfield. "She doesn't mind the lurcher so I expect it's Hector's size." And the fact that he's chased her, Mory thought.

"Your dog's a good'un, young man," said Mrs Ashfield. "Very good indeed. And so's the pony.

What's her name?" Mrs Ashfield came close and gently stroked the silky neck.

"Midnight Dancer," said Mory, unable to keep the pride from her voice.

"Well, Midnight Dancer, I'm going to ask Hector to get up and you are going to stand there and see he's as docile as any sheep. And you're not frightened of sheep are you, pretty pony?" Hector waited patiently. "Hector, stand." As the dog stood, Dancer's ears shot forward and every muscle tensed.

"It's because he chased her," said Mory unable to contain herself. "Up on the ridge."

"I know," said Mrs Ashfield. "It was a silly mistake. I thought it might keep you all at bay. In fact it aroused your interest. I realize I can't keep the hills to myself and now I'm not sure I want to."

She stroked Dancer's neck and then went to Hector and gave him a pat. Mrs Ashfield walked the big dog closer, sent him off again and walked him right round the pony. At last Dancer relaxed a little, she even let her interest move elsewhere for a brief moment. Then suddenly she stopped bothering. Mory leaned over and gave her some pony nuts.

"Well, that's better," said Mrs Ashfield and let Hector decide things for himself. Dancer didn't flinch. Lionel let Ben go and the two dogs romped together between the trees.

"Yes, it is," said Mory, stroking and patting her pony. "Thank you."

Mrs Ashfield smiled.

"I think that makes us friends," she said. "And it's time I went and you too. It wouldn't do to get caught out by the dark." Neither child said anything. "You are going home, aren't you?"

"Oh, yes," said Mory.

"And what about you, young man?" Lionel said nothing. "Do I deduce that silence means no?"

"My Dad don't know about the dog. Her Uncle wants to shoot him. I gotta keep out the way 'til the dog what done it is caught."

"That's done what?"

"Killed a sheep," said Mory.

"You can't stay out here by yourself young man. Your parents will be worried."

"I already bin here one night."

"His mum's dead." Bewildered Mrs Ashfield wondered what she was getting involved in.

"No," she said. "I simply can't leave you. Goodness me, what a drama. Now, collect what you want. You're coming with me." Lionel looked desperate.

"My Dad was away last night. He don't know."

"All the more reason to get home before he finds out." Giving herself time to think Mrs Ashfield tapped her lips with a finger. "I'll look after Ben if that's what's worrying you." It was an abrupt offer and left Lionel astonished. Hector and Ben were playing a mad game of chase, rushing backwards and forwards through the stream.

"Will you? Keep him real safe? Don't let him get shot?"

"What have I let myself in for? Yes, I will. I'll do my very best for him." Lionel looked to Mory.

"It's better than him being tied up at Penyworlod or locked up in school most of the time," she said.

"How do I know I can trust you?" said Lionel. "You could tell Mr Morgan it was him that done the sheep to get your dog off the hook."

"Yes, I could. I could do all sorts of evil things but I won't. I give you my word." She held out her hand. Lionel stared long and hard, she held his gaze and waited. Slowly Lionel took the offered hand and they shook.

It didn't take them long to get going. Mory's rucksack remained unpacked and Lionel wanted to leave the den intact. Mory didn't blame him; he'd worked hard to make it. Lionel rolled up his blanket and they tied it to Dancer's saddle with baler twine. Mory would keep it safe.

"Where's your bike?" she asked.

"In the ditch by the road. Was the safest place." Mrs Ashfield chivvied them along. Lionel was reluctant to leave but Mory was glad. Now the light was fading, the camp felt desolate and was no place for a young boy on his own. Anything might happen. Mory looked at her watch.

"I'll have to go on," she said. Already she had cut it

fine and wanted to avoid trouble.

"Yes, you go. You mustn't be out after dark either, young lady."

"Okay, Lionel?"

"Okay," he replied.

With a wave Mory set off, trotting to the foot of the gully. Behind her she heard whistling as the dogs were called in. Something was settled. Lionel had an ally and Mory knew Mrs Ashfield would be a good one. What a relief! She could go home and tell the whole story – no more secrets.

The thing that marred everything was that somewhere was a dog that killed and until that dog was found Uncle Glyn was on the war path and no other dog, good or bad, was safe from his gun.

With sure-footed ease Dancer picked her way up the gully. A chill wind blew from the ridge behind which gathered a mass of dark cloud. Soon it would rain. Lionel would have got drenched it he'd stayed. Dancer extended into a ground-covering trot. Soon they were over the ridge and hurrying past Hill Farm where they met the first drops of rain.

"We're going to get wet," Mory said. "Let's go."

It pelted as they approached the rock crop. There Mory slowed, remembering the white van. After the rocks they were off again, wind and rain in their faces, tears streaming, ears whistling, they galloped the ridge in the fading light. They reached the cattle grid gate and Mory flung herself off. Hurrying Dancer through, she led her trotting into the Llangabby yard.

"There you are," said Cara. "Where have you been?"

"I've got something to tell you," said Mory breathlessly. "I couldn't before but I can now."

"That's all very well but Aunt Sheila's in the kitchen spitting venom. We've been looking for you for hours."

"Oh, not again," said Mory, leading her hot pony into a stable. "Can I borrow your sweat rug?"

"You're just about the limit," said Cara. "All right, I'll get it."

Mory untacked Dancer and gave her a pat.

"Good pony," she said. The ride back had been fantastic.

"Guess what," said Cara flinging the sweat rug across Dancer. "Mab found the dead sheep. It was buried."

"Where?" said Mory.

"Somewhere on the other side of the ridge past the rocks."

"Heck! Who did that?"

"Well, I think it rules out Mrs Ashfield and Lionel, don't you?"

"Why?"

"Because Lionel was with you and Mrs Ashfield wouldn't have been strong enough to carry a dead sheep that far. She's too old."

"What does Uncle Glyn think?"

"He doesn't know what to think."

"Because it wasn't either of them."

"Mory, spill the beans!"

"Talking of beans," said Mory, "my back's aching like anything." She wriggled out of her rucksack, letting it fall before collapsing herself onto the soft welcoming straw.

"What's in that?"

"Baked beans and cat food amongst other things. Hang on a mo and I'll tell you everything."

"Tell me now or I'll tickle you to death."

"All right, all right." Mory lay flat out, feeling incredibly tired. "I could go to sleep right now," she sighed.

"No chance."

"Okay, okay. Shall I start at the beginning?"

"You better had."

"Well it all began with the fallen oak or rather me falling off there. I felt so stupid that I wanted to go back and jump it on my own but Lionel said he'd help me. That made it great because that way I could give you a surprise when I could jump it all right. The trouble was that Ben gave some sheep a little chase while Lionel was waiting for me and I couldn't go anyway 'cos mum made me buy trainers and Uncle Glyn saw."

"So it *was* Ben."

"Just that teeny once. It was the only time. Lionel's really trained him now. You should see. Only when

Ben rushed into the yard like that yesterday and Uncle Glyn was so furious Lionel got really scared that Ben would get shot so he ran away."

"Honest?"

"But it's okay 'cos his dad doesn't know and Mrs Ashfield is going to look after Ben. Oh, and I can jump the log. I did it lots. There, now you know everything." Mory flopped back with a sigh. "Absolutely everything."

"Hang on a minute," said Cara. "What about that letter?"

"From Lionel. Telling me to meet him and asking me not to tell anyone. That was the hard bit because I wanted to tell you and I couldn't."

"I see," said Cara, "or at least I think I do. I'm a bit confused. How did Mrs Ashfield get in on the scene?"

"We met her. Out in the hills. She found us. Lionel made this fantastic den but Hector sniffed us out and anyway Dancer was tied to a tree so it was obvious really."

Cara could see she wasn't going to get much more than this garbled story for the moment.

"How about getting your pony a feed? And you're going to have to think of something to tell your mum."

"I'll tell her about Ben. I know she feels sorry for Lionel."

"Who wouldn't with a dad like that?"

"But she also feels sorry for Caroline Spencer. That I can't understand." Dancer blew warm breath down Mory's neck. "All right, all right, I'm going."

"She's not so bad when you get her on your own."

"I'm glad you think so," said Mory cuddling Dancer's soft nose. "I wish I did." She heaved herself up, duty bound to go to the tack room for a scoopful of pony nuts.

# ELEVEN

# *Half Term*

Next morning at school everything seemed back to normal. Lionel came pedalling along the lane, rearing to a stop, to be greeted by Mory, Cara and Josh at the gate.

"Everything all right?" Mory asked. Lionel, taken aback by the reception committee, gave one of his nods. They made way for him to push his bike to the shed. "So what happened?" Mory asked. "Did you get home before your dad?"

"She took me."

"All the way?"

"Bike in the back."

"Megan and Ian were really worried. You never said you were taking Ben and when you didn't bring him back they phoned Aunt Olwen. They even tried your dad."

"I'll go round after school."

"Don't worry, Aunt Olwen's told them you're safe and that Mrs Ashfield's got Ben."

"I couldn't phone from home. Dad came back."

"Can we see your den?" Josh asked.

"If you like."

Mory had had to explain everything about Lionel and Ben to her mum and Aunt Olwen. They'd already had Megan's phone call so knew something was up. It stopped them being cross at once.

"Is Mrs Ashfield going to keep looking after Ben?" Cara asked.

"She never said for definite. Him an' Hector get on real well. An' she give me this." Lionel pulled out a collar.

"An old one of Hector's. Proper wide one. I cut it smaller. Just right for a lurcher she says."

"What is a lurcher exactly?" asked Mory. "She called Ben that yesterday."

"Something that lurches, of course," said Josh angling himself sideways.

"Pack it in, you," said Lionel good humouredly. "I never heard of them 'til she said. They're a cross breed. She says from the size of him, Ben's probably whippet cross border collie. It can be greyhound cross rough collie to get a bigger dog."

"Is Hector a big one?" Josh asked interested.

"No, a deer hound."

"Does he catch deer?" Mory asked.

"They did in olden days, not now."

"Mory says Ben's brilliant with sheep," said Josh. "Must be the collie in him."

"To look you'd never say he had collie," said

Lionel. "Whippet yes. He's got the long fur of a collie but that's the wrong colour. Still, I ain't complaining. I like 'im as he is." Lionel stuffed the collar back in his pocket and unclipped his polythene bag.

"Wait 'til I train Nip," said Josh. "We can work sheep together."

"Fat chance," said Lionel. "Ben'll never get near Llangabby without being shot."

"I wish the sheep killer was found," said Cara. "Dad's going everywhere with his gun. I'm scared he'll shoot the wrong dog."

"He'll shoot any dog," said Lionel ruefully. "People better watch out."

Josh had promised to take a photograph of Mory jumping the log after school. Mory, Cara and Sarah sat at their table discussing it before assembly. Caroline listened to the three girls opposite.

"I suppose you think a photograph will prove something," she said at last.

"It's not for proof," said Cara, quickly. "We all know Dancer can jump. It's for art!" She didn't quite know why she said that but the effect on Caroline was electric.

"Art," she scoffed. "None of you would know one end of a paint brush from another."

"Equestrian art," said Cara. "It's not just that Dancer can jump but it's how she does it. It's to study her style."

"And we can manage it on our own without you

thank you very much," said Sarah.

Mory was impressed. She'd never have thought anything like that and it gave her time to catch hold of her temper, and a row was avoided in spite of her feelings being hurt.

Later all that was forgotten when Mory was actually cantering round the fallen oak bringing Dancer in for the first jump. Josh had his camera focused and his finger poised. Mory saw the strides, one, two, three and they were in the air. Click went the shutter. Josh wound the film on. Round they came again. One, two, three, click.

"One more for luck," shouted Josh.

"I'll go the other way," cried Mory turning Dancer.

"We'll do it downhill."

Round they came again.

"Steady, girl," said Mory. One, two, three and they were in the air. It was a terrific jump. Cara cheered.

"Got it," cried Josh. "That should mean at least one good one."

"Anyone else want to jump?" Mory asked.

"I will," said Cara handing Rustler's reins to Mory. "That was quite something."

"Get Cara!" shouted Mory. Josh lined up the shot.

Cara came at a steady canter. The approach was perfect but at the last moment Misty stopped. Cara was nearly unseated, his refusal was so unexpected. The camera clicked anyway.

"Bother," said Josh.

"What happened?" cried Mory.

"Something caught his eye. I don't know what it was. I'm coming in again."

This time Cara was firmer with her approach and Misty jumped the tree perfectly. Again the shutter clicked.

"Got it," said Josh. "How about someone taking one of me?"

"I will," said Mory.

While Misty jumped the tree downhill Josh handed his camera to Mory. She waited while Josh trotted some circles to loosen Rustler up.

"Okay," he cried. "Here we go!" Mory held the camera steady and as Rustler came off the ground clicked the shutter button.

"Got it," she cried. "Brilliant, Josh."

"I hope so," he called back. "That was the last picture."

"Great," said Mory. "That means it can be developed straight away."

"Yeah," said Josh trotting over, patting his pony. "Dad can take them in tomorrow. Mum can pick them up on Friday."

"Perfect," said Mory.

"Home time," said Cara.

"Okay," said Mory, "but I want to ride up to Hill Farm and thank Mrs Ashfield. She's been so nice to Lionel."

"Your heart-throb," teased Cara.

"Shut up, you."

"We'll go on," said Josh hanging his camera over his back. "Meet you by the rocks."

Mory made her way up to the house. Mrs Ashfield's Range Rover wasn't there. The only vehicle parked by the gate was the white van.

"Hells bell's," said Mory.

She stood for a moment until a creepy feeling made her want to get away. Was it something about the van or maybe just being there on her own? Either way she turned quickly and cantered up the track after the others.

That night Mory sat at her table and gazed dreamily at her pictures. On Friday she would have the longed-for jumping photograph. She could almost see it on the wall. Dad was taking the film to be developed and had it tucked safely with his wallet. Josh had printed a large notice – DON'T FORGET FILM – which was sitting in the car to remind him.

Mory wanted the picture badly. Once on show with the others she was convinced nothing would stop her jumping a clear round in the show jumping. She'd done it tonight when they'd got back. Cara had insisted that she go round the mini practice course in the paddock. Dancer had jumped each jump without hesitation – the parallel, the wall, the lurid yellow and green poles – and she hadn't bucked once.

"Yes," said Mory, stroking Splodge's thick fur as he

lay a curled bundle on her lap. "I think I'm in with a chance."

Instructions for the dressage test lay in front of her.

"But how I'm ever going to remember this I don't know." But she wasn't worried. If she went wrong in the test, too bad. It was the show jumping that counted.

The next day in school Mory waited for Lionel as usual. He arrived with a big grin on his face.

"You look like the cat that got the cream," she said.

"You'll never guess what she did." He meant Mrs Ashfield. "She told my dad off." Mory knew that would be quite a feat. "Honest. And he says yes, Mrs an' no, Mrs an' three bags full, Mrs like she was queen or something. She tells about Ben. I nearly dies. But he says, okay, Mrs, he can keep the dog. She makes some sort of deal with him. They shake an' that's it. He was never nasty after she went nor nothing. An' when he goes off I'm to stay with her or any friends that'll have me."

"Does that mean you can keep Ben at home?" Lionel nodded.

"Too right. That Mrs is brilliant. I got to keep buying his food an' everythink. But that's all right."

"And you can stay with us. Mum and Dad always let us have friends to stay. We did lots when we lived in Waring." Lionel looked quite overcome so Mory changed the subject.

"Have you been inside Hill Farm yet?" she asked. Lionel came alive again.

"You should see it, Mory. It's pictures everywhere. Dogs and horses. Birds. That's what she does. An' she's good."

"I wish I could see right now," said Mory, wide-eyed. "Fancy Mrs Ashfield being a real artist. What a wonderful surprise." Lionel laughed.

"You will. Sure as eggs is eggs." And with his polythene bag slung over his shoulder Lionel walked with Mory into school.

The rest of the week flew by with half-term excitement in the air. Sheila was under strict instructions not to forget the photographs when she shopped in Aberdawl on Friday. Mory told her she would die if she did.

"I almost believe it," Sheila had said. It was on her shopping list and Mory had underlined it in red.

When school was finally over it was a great release. A whole week stretched before them of riding and practice and then the Penyworlod Show. When the bus stopped Mory, Josh and Cara leapt from it, liberating themselves with cries of FREEDOM, FREEDOM! as if escaping from some terrible prison and not just school.

"See you in a minute," was Mory's cry to Cara at the Llangabby gate, a cry left hanging in air, she and Josh were gone so fast.

The pelting feet brought David from the pottery.

"Want any tea?" he asked.

"No, thanks Dad, we're going to build a handy pony course. Have it later."

"How about you, Josh?"

"It's okay Dad. Aunt Olwen'll give us something if we're hungry." David laughed.

"Half-term fever, eh? Well, I think I can trust you not to starve." And he went back in the pottery, leaving his children to rush off and change.

Indoors, sitting on the middle of the kitchen table were two tins of paint in front of which was a piece of paper which said, "For Mory. My birthday paint, Love, Dad."

"Oh, great," said Mory and read, "Non Drip Silk Black" on one tin and "Non Drip Silk Petal Yellow" on the other. "For the moon," cried Mory. "Isn't Dad clever?"

"What's clever?" said Josh, flinging his sandwich box in the sink.

"Getting me moon paint for my Midnight Dancer mural."

"S'pose so," said Josh. "What do we need to take up for the handy pony course?"

"Oh, a black dustbin bag," said Mory. "Old clothes for a washing line. We've got to practise getting on and off the wrong side. Sometimes they make you do that. And … I can't think of anything else right now." Mory flung her sandwich box in the sink and dumped her rucksack on a peg in the hall. "I'm going to feed Splodge." Josh ran up to his room to change. A few minutes later they collided on the stairs.

"I'm going on up. I want to see the puppies," Josh said.

"I'll follow you up as fast as I can."

In the silence after Josh's clattering a distant crack echoed from some far place out in the hills. Was it gunshot? No other sound followed and Mory wondered if she'd imagined it. Then rushing to change she forgot it.

When Mory panted into the paddock, Cara had already laid a blue sheet on the ground and weighted it with small rocks.

"For them to walk over. Sometimes you get something like this."

"Can we use two of the big plastic drums?" Mory asked. "I thought we could move the black polythene bag from the top of one to the other. I'll fill the bag with some hay."

"That's a good one," said Cara. "I've hung a washing line from the tree in the hedge to that jump stand." She pointed it out. "I haven't got any washing on it yet." Josh arrived with some clothes pegs. Cara began pushing in some of Aunt Olwen's bamboo canes for bending sticks for the ponies to weave in and out of.

"And we've got to practise for the flag race."

"Heck," said Mory. "I forgot to ask Lionel if he'd be in our team."

"Don't bother," said Cara. "Mum says we've got to do it with Caroline."

"Oh, no!" The "no" out a great wail of fed-upness. That was nothing to the singing of the cattle grid and the screech of tyres as the Landrover came to an urgent stop in the yard. They looked at one another and ran. Aunt Olwen was already there, a hand on Uncle Glyn's arm, concerned by his white set face.

"That dog's done it again," he said flinging open the back door of the Landrover. "I got a shot at it but it went off towards the forestry. Heaven knows where it comes from." Mab jumped down. She had been sitting next to the torn body of a dead lamb. Mory put her hands over her face.

"Poor little thing," she whispered. But even with eyes tight closed she could still see the blood-splattered lamb lying dead on the Landrover floor. She remembered the distant crack; it was gunshot she had heard. If only the dog had been frightened off before it had killed the lamb.

"Come on children, off you go," said Aunt Olwen ushering them out of the way. "It's dead. Nothing can be done for it."

Uncle Glyn's a good shepherd. He cares for his sheep, thought Mory. The dog's running free. Free dogs turn wild and wild dogs kill. Why won't they stop it?

Cara linked her arm through Mory's and the three of them went back to finish building the course. But it wasn't the same now. When Sheila went by in the car Mory decided to go home. The handy pony course could wait. Looking at the photographs might make her less sad. The others felt the same and they set off down the track to Black Rock.

# TWELVE

## *A Clue*

They looked pretty glum when they trooped into the kitchen.

"What a lot of long faces," said Sheila. "Whatever's the matter?"

"Dad's found a dead lamb," said Cara. "He's just brought it home."

"Ripped apart," said Mory. "It was horrible."

"Poor little thing," said Sheila, giving Mory a hug.

"I just wish we could find the dog and stop it before it gets shot," cried Mory. "I mean, some stupid owner isn't controlling it."

"I know, I know," said Sheila. "It's causing a lot of distress. Uncle Glyn must be very upset."

"Mum, why does its owner let it?" Josh asked.

"Perhaps they don't realize," said Sheila. "Although that's probably unlikely. So I don't know." Sheila went to her bag on the table. "Here, I didn't forget. The photographs! Let's cheer ourselves up with these." Sheila put them on the table. "Anyone want a drink?"

"Bagsie me have cola." said Josh.

"And me," said Cara.

"Can I have hot chocolate?" said Mory. "And bagsie me have the photos."

"Hey Mory, they're mine." Josh snatched them from her.

"Well go on then. Open them."

"Josh, they're all puppies and Mab," said Cara.

"No, they're not. The pony ones are at the bottom."

"Can we look at the puppy ones second?" pleaded Mory. Josh got to the jumping photographs. "Wow, Josh, that's brilliant." He held it up. Mory and Dancer were flying above the fallen oak.

"Darling, that's a wonderful jump," said Sheila putting two glasses of cola on the table.

"I've been practising. I didn't tell you but the first time Dancer jumped that oak tree I fell off."

"I'm glad you didn't," said Sheila with a grimace.

"She jumped it big, that's why," said Mory.

"How about this one?" said Josh, holding up the picture of Dancer jumping downhill.

"That's the one," said Mory. "Can I have that one?" Josh handed it over. "Thanks a million."

"They came out really well. Even this one," said Josh, holding up Misty's refusal for all to see.

"I don't want to look," said Cara.

"I'm amazed you didn't come off," said Sheila. "You look half off in the picture."

"Bet I would have," said Mory. "Just shows you how good she is."

"Just don't let me see it," wailed Cara.

"Okay," said Mory and tucked the offending photo underneath the one Josh had given her. "Look at this one instead. It's wicked." Cara gave it a glance.

"You can have it if you like," said Josh handing it to her. She took it shyly.

"What about the one I took of you, Josh?" Mory asked. "Oh, not bad, eh?"

"Well," said Sheila, "looks like I'm breeding a family of show jumpers. You have all been busy."

"It's practice," said Mory, then remembered. "You know what Aunt Olwen's done? She says we've got to have Caroline Spencer in our flag race team. We wanted Lionel."

"Have you talked to Olwen about it?"

Mory shook her head. "Cara told me."

"I think she was hoping you might ask Caroline as she doesn't seem to have many riding friends," said Sheila.

"But Caroline hates me. It's bad enough that she's in our riding school class," said Mory.

"Then you'd better to talk to Olwen and make it clear how you feel," said Sheila.

"If I must. But tomorrow. Now I'm going to pin my picture up, learn my dressage test and plan my mural for Dad."

Upstairs, sitting at her table, Mory spent ages gazing at the photograph as if she couldn't quite believe it.

She rummaged for some pins and whilst trying to decide where to pin it the picture of Misty's refusal slipped from the back. Smiling she picked it up. Cara was all bottom, legs and arms.

"How did she stay on?" sighed Mory.

"Determination," said Josh, his head round the door. "And grip!"

"Look, what do you think?" asked Mory, holding the photograph against the wall.

"Great photograph taken by yours truly. Yeah, it looks good there." Mory stuck in a pin.

"That refusal was impressive," said Josh picking up the other photograph. "It was odd that he refused, wasn't it?"

"Not like him at all," Mory agreed. "Something distracted him."

"Yes, I wonder what it was. Look at that daylight between Cara and the saddle."

"I know. I can't understand why she didn't fall off."

"Amazing. Hey, what's that behind Misty's tail? That shape in the heather. That's what he's looking at. It's the back of a dog. There's the tail, see? The rest's hidden behind Misty. He must have seen it before it went behind those rocks." Once the shape was pointed out it was obvious.

"Heck," said Mory. "It *is* a dog! That means it could be *the* dog."

"Yes," said Josh. "But where does it come from?"

"If it is *the* dog that definitely lets out Ben and

Hector. It's nothing like them," cried Mory. Then it occurred to her that this had happened near Hill Farm. "I think we should show Mrs Ashfield," she said. "She could keep a look out for the dog."

"Why her? I think Uncle Glyn should see it."

"No," said Mory. "Don't let's say anything to Uncle Glyn yet."

"But Mory …"

"No, really. He might do something terrible if he got angry. Let's show Mrs Ashfield first. She's brilliant. She'll know what to do. Keep a secret?"

"I don't know."

"Please," begged Mory. "Please. If she can't help then we'll show Uncle Glyn. Promise."

Josh sighed. "Oh, all right." Mory spat on her palm and after a bit Josh spat on his and they shook.

"Right, we'll get up at six."

"Six!"

"All right, half past but we mustn't miss our chance. There's a lot to do. Handy pony practice, our riding lesson." They spat and shook again.

"Early bed then," said Josh. "Up at first cock crow."

"Except we haven't got one," said Mory. "Thank goodness for alarm clocks."

Next morning Mory and Josh were tacked up and ready to go by half past seven. The Llangabby farm house was quiet. Even Uncle Glyn didn't seem to be up early this morning. Mory left an explanatory note in the tack room for Cara before they stole out of the yard and led their ponies through the gate by the cattle grid. Mab watched them go.

It promised to be a fine day, a haze obscured the view but the sky was clear above.

"I hope this is the right thing to do," said Josh.

"Yes," said Mory. She had the photograph tucked in her pocket. "I know it is."

The ponies walked out briskly and soon were trotting to the rock crop. The sun creeping up the sky made long shadows in front of the rocks.

"It's still a bit early," said Josh. "Do you think we're going to wake her?"

"I hadn't thought of that," said Mory.

Coming down to Hill Farm smoke drifted up from the chimney.

"She's awake," said Mory. "The fire's lit." Josh wasn't sure that proved anything.

When they arrived Mory dismounted and handed over Dancer's reins. The gate had been mended and swung open easily. She went up the narrow path to the front door. There was no knocker or letter-box. She knocked as hard as her knuckles would allow. Hector's bark was instantaneous but it was some time before the door was opened and Mrs Ashfield's surprised face looked out.

"This is an early call," she said.

"I've got something to show you."

"You'd better come in. Do you want to tie the ponies up?"

"No, it's all right, Josh'll hold them."

Mory went inside. Hector sniffed her and gave her a lick. She stroked his shaggy head. Mory was offered a chair and sat down obediently. A bowl of fruit was on the table and the room smelt of toast. Mrs Ashfield was having breakfast.

"I'm sorry it's so early," said Mory, "but I had to come. Uncle Glyn's had a lamb killed."

A frown formed on the elderly face. "And he's going to accuse me?" Mrs Ashfield asked.

"I don't think so. But I wanted you to see this." Mory pulled the photograph from her pocket. "There's a strange dog behind Misty. That's what Misty's looking at. See? You can just make it out."

Mrs Ashfield put on her spectacles and took the photograph to the window.

"Did your cousin come a cropper?"

"No, she stayed on." Mory looked quickly round the room. It was just as Lionel had said, full of pictures. Eagerly Mory noted the easel and small table covered with brushes and paints. She saw ponies, dogs, an owl, a buzzard, hill creatures bursting from their canvases. They were perfect. She longed to get up and look properly but didn't dare.

"Can I keep this?" Mrs Ashfield asked tapping the photograph on her finger. "Someone has lied to me."

Mory, startled, stared up at the imposing, tweed-clad figure.

"Please, if you know whose dog it is, don't let Uncle Glyn shoot it."

"Leave it with me, Mory. May I keep the photograph for the time being?"

"Yes."

"It'll be a great help." It was dismissal. Mrs Ashfield led the way to the door.

"Thank you for being so nice to Lionel," said Mory impulsively. "And for standing up to his dad." She wasn't sure she should have said that. Mrs Ashfield's severe face stared down at her.

"The boy has a gift with animals," she said. "I hope it doesn't go to waste." But it wasn't Lionel she was thinking about as she tapped the photograph.

"He's a brilliant rider," said Mory. "It's a shame he can't have a pony of his own. It doesn't seem fair."

"No," said Mrs Ashfield soberly. "I don't suppose his father could afford it even if he wanted to. But he's lucky to have a friend like you." Mory went pink. That was it then. She hurried outside.

"She's going to sort it," she told Josh.

"I hope so," he said. "Because I still think we should have shown Uncle Glyn first." They turned their ponies and set off back to Llangabby with Mory wondering if she'd done the right thing.

# THIRTEEN

## *Culprit*

Cara was miffed that she didn't see the photograph and complained about it being left with Mrs Ashfield.

"Well, you wouldn't look at it when we did have it," said Mory.

"But it's our evidence and now you've given it away."

"Mrs Ashfield won't keep it," said Mory. "She's going to use it to sort everything out."

"You hope!"

Cara's irritation caused a twinge of doubt. No, Mrs Ashfield was as good as her word. Mory trusted her.

"Well, it's too late now," she said. "We'll just have to wait and see."

"Come on," said Josh. "There's no point in arguing. Let's practise."

The handy pony course was not as easy as Mory expected. She asked Dancer to cross the blue sheet and she refused. Urged on, she cat-jumped it. Misty and Rustler gave her a lead and she trod on it then leapt across in a panic, bumping into Rustler.

"Watch out," cried Josh, indignant.

"Sorry."

Mory gave her some pony nuts for bravery and tried again. After a few more goes Dancer walked across without spooking or rushing. She was slightly better with the black rubbish bag, seemingly quite happy to go up to it, but she shied when Mory picked it up. This made Mory drop it, startling Dancer enough to set her bucking.

"I don't think I've got a Handy Pony," Mory said, exasperated, as she regained control. "She didn't like the rustling."

"Don't expect too much," said Cara. "She's not an old hand like the others. She's got it all to learn."

"You're right, I'm being impatient. Could you put the bag back on the barrel? I'll see if she'll go back up to it."

Dancer wasn't quite sure what to make of the black bag now but eventually she went close enough to sniff it and stayed to eat pony nuts.

"That's enough for now," Mory said. "We've got a whole week to practise and anyway you're a handy enough pony for me as you are." After all they had a lesson to go to later. It was time Dancer had a rest.

Aunt Olwen asked Mory to sit next to her when she drove them to Penyworlod for the lesson.

"I was wondering if you would ask Caroline to be

in your team for the flag race," said her aunt, missing Mory's pained expression by turning into the lane. "As you have your lessons together I thought it might be nice."

"I wanted Lionel to be in our team."

"Have you asked him?"

"Not yet."

"So you could ask Caroline?" said Aunt Olwen.

"But Caroline hates me," said Mory in protesting tones.

"I'm sure she doesn't," said Aunt Olwen. "But it was only a suggestion. I'll leave it with you."

Some suggestion! Mory didn't want to displease her aunt but she wanted Lionel in their team.

"Besides if we ask Caroline who will Lionel go with?" she said.

"Everyone'll want Lionel," said Cara from the back. "He's so good." Mory sighed and gave up. She distracted herself by unfolding a crumpled copy of the dressage test. Better to learn the test than think about Caroline Spencer and how fed up she was with Aunt Olwen and her suggestion.

Today's lesson was a double one to make up for not having one the Saturday before the show, when Megan and Ian would be getting everything ready. They started with exercises and schooled the ponies at walk and trot and canter. Then Megan asked them each to ride their dressage test. Cara went first and rode Misty in a relaxed and fluid way, remembering every movement.

It was good and Mory was impressed. Megan was pleased too but still had a list of things for Cara to work on.

Josh went second and trotted into the school, leaving an empty space between Mory and Caroline. If the dreaded flag race question was going to be asked it was now or never.

"Caroline."

"What!"

Mory swallowed and hesitated at the unfriendly voice. "Would you like to be in our flag race team?" She got it out.

"Me? In your flag race team? You must be joking," sneered Caroline. The words hurt and were a relief at the same time.

"Fine," said Mory turning away. Caroline was ungracious, ungrateful and a stuck-up pig.

"I shan't be playing any silly games with Doughnut. I'm going to concentrate on what really counts, the dressage and show jumping." Mory caught the smirk. "I shall leave the silly stuff to people like you." Mory knew better than to reply but she was off the hook. She looked at Josh and Rustler trotting in a twenty-metre circle and blotted out Caroline and her put-down words.

It was a relief to catch sight of Lionel. Mory rode over to him and Ben at his heel wagged his tail.

"I've been wanting to ask you. Will you be in our team for the flag race?"

"I'll be riding Tawney. He's not good for that sort of thing."

"I don't care," said Mory.

"Then yes, if you want." Mory was delighted. Much better to have Lionel who would throw himself into it even if Tawney did misbehave.

"And," said Mory, significantly. "We've photographed the killer dog! Mrs Ashfield's got the picture. I've got a feeling she might know whose dog it is."

"If she does she'll sort it."

"Mory!" It was her turn to do the test.

"I know she will. And when she does you'll be able to bring Ben up to us," said Mory, turning Dancer. "Don't watch this. It'll be terrible."

It wasn't. Apart from going wrong four times the walking, trotting and cantering were Dancer at her best. Mory was finding it easier and easier to help Dancer move from pace to pace and to turn in balance. If only she could keep the whole test in her head. There was so much to remember all at once. But Megan was pleased in spite of the mistakes and Mory loved the good feeling of being in harmony with her pony. It could only get better.

Lionel helped put up the jumps. He and Megan made a small course and Dancer excelled herself. No bucks, no rushing, a nice steady rhythm. They knocked down one jump when Mory made too sharp a turn but it didn't matter. Aglow, Mory hugged her.

"You're wonderful, wonderful," Mory whispered into her mane.

As the lesson came to an end Mory realized Sheila and David were at the side of the school watching.

"Did you see us jump?" she asked.

"Did you?" Josh chorused.

"We certainly did," said David, pushing Rustler's investigating nose away from his pocket before giving him a mint.

"Mum, Dancer was wonderful," said Mory. "Absolutely wonderful."

"She was," agreed Sheila. "You're real partners."

"Yes, that's exactly what we are."

"And now," said David, "we're going to help you spend some money."

"Riding clothes!" said Mory. "I nearly forgot."

The excitement of new jodhpurs and jodhpur boots, a second-hand but not too worn hacking jacket and the thrill of a successful lesson kept Mory's mind in a whirl as they drove back to Llangabby. But as soon as they turned into the yard everything evaporated at the sight of Uncle Glyn's angry face. He was waiting for them, his shotgun across his arm.

"I want the Landrover," he said grimly. "I've seen the dog in the back of that plumber's van on its way out to Hill Farm. Now's my chance."

They hurried to unload the ponies so that Uncle Glyn could unhitch the trailer. Mory's mind raced. A dog in the back of the plumber's van! Of course! How stupid she had been not to realize. The plumber had a dog! But Mrs Ashfield knew that. Of course she did. Serve the plumber right, then. But it wasn't the plumber who was going to get shot. Mory remembered the dead sheep and the dead lamb. Beside them came a picture of a dead dog. A dog like Mab or Hector or Ben. She couldn't bear it. It wasn't the dog's fault it hadn't been trained properly; it was the plumber's. Was there time to give a warning? She must try.

"Josh, hold Dancer for me," she said. Dancer's rug was off in a trice and her saddle on. As Uncle Glyn swung the trailer out of the way Mory grabbed her bridle from the Landrover. She put it on over the headcollar.

"What are you doing?" said Josh under his breath.

Mory tightened the girth. The words *I've got to save the dog* thudded through her brain.

"I'm going to warn them," she said. Her hat was in the Landrover.

"Out of the way, Mory," said Uncle Glyn closing the door before she could get it.

"I've got to save the dog," she told Josh. Her tone was urgent.

"How can you? He's dead meat!"

"I can try and get there first. Open the cattle grid gate for me."

"Mory, you can't!"

The Landrover engine roared. "Then I'll jump it."

Mory swung herself into the saddle. The Landrover sped out of the yard and with a clatter of hooves Mory followed.

"Mory, come back!" shouted Aunt Olwen. "You're not wearing a hat."

It didn't matter. Without thinking of the danger Mory trotted out of the yard and eyed the gate. She broke into a canter, saw the stride and urged Dancer forward. The pony went without hesitation. The gate came to them, stride, stride, stride, and with hocks under her, Dancer leapt into the air, clearing it by

centimetres. With thoughts only of catching up the bumping, lurching, Landrover Mory set off at a thunderous pace leaving a sea of astonished faces behind her.

It was a lot to ask the pony. She'd worked hard all day but Mory was compelled. Her mind raced against more bloodshed, against the town man with his un-curbed dog and Uncle Glyn, the guardian of his sheep.

Dancer went like the wind. By the rock crop the Landrover slowed. They were right behind it. Mory cut down from the rocks and looped in front, urging Dancer on down the slope. Now she could see the white van and the Range Rover. They were there,

Mrs Ashfield, the man and his dog, not knowing. She looked back and saw Uncle Glyn, furious, waving at her and rode on.

"Mrs Ashfield!" she yelled as loud as her lungs could manage. "Mrs Ashfield!" Inside the van a dog barked. It was joined by barking from the house and behind her came the roar of the Landrover.

"Mrs Ashfield!"

The door took an age to open. Dancer panted and pranced. Mory ran a gentling hand along her soaked neck.

"Uncle Glyn's coming and he knows." Her voice was urgent, hoarse. "He's mad and he's got a gun."

"Thank you," said Mrs Ashfield with astonishing calm. "Mr Griffiths and I were on our way to see him. He's saved us the trouble."

Mrs Ashfield walked down the little path and opened the gate. Mr Griffiths, the plumber, hesitated then followed.

"Will the dog be safe?" Mory asked.

"I expect so," said Mrs Ashfield.

"He can't go round shooting other people's dogs," said the plumber uneasily.

"He wants to protect his sheep," said Mrs Ashfield. "Wouldn't you?"

The Landrover came to an untidy halt and Uncle Glyn jumped from it swinging his gun across his arm, barrel down.

"Mory, go home," he said.

"Please, don't shoot it," said Mory. "Please, Uncle Glyn." Her pleas were overridden by Mrs Ashfield's steady voice.

"We were on our way to see you, Mr Morgan. This is Huw Griffiths. Mr Griffith, this is Glyn Morgan from Llangabby Farm. The dead sheep belonged to him."

"How do," said the plumber. His discomfort was obvious. "The dog was only playing. She got it down before I could stop her. I thought you wouldn't miss the one. The lamb was a mistake. She got out. Sorry." He tentatively held out his hand and withdrew it again. "I apologize."

"Apologize!" said Uncle Glyn, menace oozing from each syllable of the word. "Your dog has killed a sheep and a lamb and no doubt terrorized the rest with chasing and you apologize. Not good enough."

"I'll pay, no problem."

"Oh, yes," said Uncle Glyn. "You'll pay or I'll have the law on you." Drawing in a breath he turned to Mrs Ashfield. "I owe you an apology, Mrs Ashfield."

"And I you for being a foolish, trusting old woman. But the proof is in this photograph and once seen can hardly be denied."

Uncle Glyn took the photograph. He gave it a long, hard look and turned to Mory.

"Why didn't you tell me?"

"To stop you shooting it. The dog didn't know it was doing wrong," said Mory. "That makes it innocent. It's the owner who should be punished, not the dog." Mory caught sight of an alert, furry face looking at them from the back of the van.

"Mory," said Uncle Glyn, "I'll shoot any dog that chases my sheep. I don't know any sheep farmer who wouldn't. But right now I'm not going to shoot anything. That's a promise. You go home and look after Dancer. Leave this to me." Mory turned to go. "Walk her back, she's sweated up badly." He turned to the plumber. "You can thank my niece for your dog's life. But if I ever see it out here again I'll shoot it on sight. Understood?" The man nodded. "You owe me and I want to see the colour of your money." The man reached into his pocket.

"How much?"

Mrs Ashfield gave Mory a reassuring smile and went indoors, leaving Mr Griffiths to pay what he owed. Mory rode slowly home.

# FOURTEEN

## *The Show*

Mory caused quite a stir amongst her family. Her belief in Hector's and Ben's innocence had been right, as events with the plumber and his dog had proved. As to jumping the cattle grid gate, even to think about it gave Sheila the "heebie jeebies" as she called it.

"And without a hat!" she repeated so often it became a family joke. Now, nobody could do anything *without a hat*! Although how she had the courage to jump the gate Mory was not sure. Looking at it in the cool calm of the following day, she was astonished at its size. Dancer hadn't thought twice. The pony had been quite confident of her ability to clear it and what ability it was turning out to be!

The killer dog mystery solved, Mory's thoughts turned to the show. The show. The show. For the whole of the half-term week nothing else was talked of. Sheila and David, remembering Dancer's heroic leap, encouraged sober jumping practice in the Llangabby paddock.

Yet when it came to practising things did not go well for Mory. Fences were knocked down, Dancer did lots of bucking and refused to go under the washing line when it had clothes on. It was very trying and still Mory could not remember her dressage test. At least, she remembered it perfectly when she walked the test but when she rode Dancer sooner or later she'd forget what came next.

The night before the show found Mory very down in the dumps.

"I don't know what's going wrong," she said to her mother. "One minute Dancer's fantastic and the next she and I can't do a thing right. She's going to be hopeless in the Handy Pony. She spooks at everything."

"Surely it's not that bad," said Sheila, doing her best to comfort. "You know she can jump."

"Yes, but I've made a mess of jumping all week."

"Maybe," said Sheila, bringing her concerned eyes level with Mory's, "just maybe you're trying too hard."

"How can I try too hard?"

"Well, sometimes, when we want to do something badly, we wind ourselves into a tight ball, and the harder we try the further we get from where we want to go. Remember when you jumped the cattle grid gate? You didn't think about it or really try – you just did it. And that's because you were thinking of saving the dog and something inside, the not trying hard to get it right part of you, took over."

"Yes," said Mory. "It was easy as winking. But I couldn't do it now."

"And neither should you."

"No, no. But I think I see what you mean. If I'm all screwed up in a tight ball it might make Dancer like that too."

"She's bound to feel when you're tense, isn't she? Just relax and enjoy riding her. It's only a show."

"It's THE show."

"No, it's not. It's the first show of many. It doesn't matter if you make a mess of it."

"It does!"

"To you it does but it won't matter to Dancer. All she wants is a relaxed rider who makes her feel comfortable and confident and lets her enjoy herself. Think of your partnership. Not just winning or being best or showing Caroline."

At the mention of Caroline Mory blushed. Of course she wanted to show that horrid girl but Sheila's words sank in and made sense. Her partnership with Dancer was more important than anything else and if that was right then everything else would come right in the end. It was to do with trust; she would trust herself and the pony.

"Thanks Mum." She gave Sheila a hug. "Thanks. You're right. I don't have to prove anything to Caroline or to anybody. Just be me."

"Just be you," said Sheila hugging her back. "And a very lovely you, you are."

Mory grinned. "I'd better go and clean my tack. The others have been doing theirs for ages."

The show morning found all three young people up bright and early. Three ponies were groomed until they gleamed, feet were picked out, tails were bandaged, manes were plaited and hooves were oiled. Clean tack was loaded into the Landrover which stood ready hitched to the trailer. Haynets were filled. While the ponies calmly munched their breakfasts amidst the hectic preparation Aunt Olwen called the young people in to munch theirs.

It seemed for ever before they set off but at last they did. This was the moment Mory had been waiting for. She sat hugging her knees, thrilling with anticipation while her <u>mother</u>'s words <u>hummed</u> in <u>her ears</u>. *Think of your partnership. Just be you.* And she would. So what if Dancer spooked or bucked or she forgot the test! She was going to enjoy it. The others bubbled with excitement, jumping up and down and giggling. When they turned into Penyworlod Mory jumped up too and burst into a cheer.

Dancer was fully aware there was something different about the day. The car park was full of horse boxes and trailers. People and ponies milled everywhere. They were taking the ponies out of the trailer when the car arrived with David, Sheila and Uncle Glyn. They were in time to see Dancer prance down the ramp, ears pricked, eyes on stalks.

"That's an excited pony," said Uncle Glyn. "Might be a handful."

"I hope Mory'll be all right," Sheila said.

"She will," Uncle Glyn said confidently. "She can cope." But Sheila remained anxious and, when Mory mounted, saw she had cause to be. Her daughter seemed to be sitting on a firework. Fortunately, Megan saw the prancing and dancing and summoned Lionel. He was riding Tawney and looking very smart. If Mory hadn't seen his freckles she would never have recognized him.

"I don't know what's got into Dancer," she said. "She's a complete lunatic."

"Excited," said Lionel. "Come up the field and we'll work her. Keep relaxed, she'll soon calm down. Push her into your hands Mory. Do that and you'll have her."

Mory did her best. It was a bit like trying to put the lid on a bouncy Jack-in-a-box. But she sat, calm, concentrated and relaxed. She held Dancer gently but firmly, hands not pulling, but giving and taking and all the time saying, "Go forward, now halt, go forward, go forward, now halt."

"That's it," said Lionel. "Nice, boring, obedience work. Make her do what she's told. She's got to respect you Mory. And listen. Not watch everything else and muck about."

"I'd never have guessed she'd be like this," said Mory.

"She's got sparkle, wants to know everything," said Lionel. "Like this one." And he ran a hand along Tawney's immaculately plaited neck. He did look beautiful. "You'd hate a dobbin. See, already she's calmer." It was true. Mory could almost feel her saying *Oh all right, if I have to*. "What time's your test?"

Mory quickly looked at her watch.

"In fifteen minutes."

"That's quick," said Lionel.

"I'm the second to go. You and the others are later."

"Trot some circles. Do lots of transitions up and down. Surprise her. Make her think." Mory set off and Lionel fired a few more instructions at her. "Go big, go small. Now change the rein. Don't rush it. Think of the rhythm." Mory did as she was told and trotted for five minutes. She timed herself. When she was ready she cantered some circles. At first Dancer got fizzy and wanted to rush off so Mory made her trot and walk again.

"That's it. You've got her now. You're boss. She does what you say."

Dancer realized this. Determination seeped through every pore of her rider and the pony began to listen. The feeling of rhythm and harmony that had eluded Mory all week came creeping back.

"You'll have to go down," said Lionel. "It's nearly time."

"Where is it?"

"In the indoor school."

"Hells bell's, Lionel, we've only been in there twice."

"So what if she spooks a bit? Ride like that. You'll be great."

"I'll forget the test," said Mory pessimistically.

"It don't matter," said Lionel. Mory grinned.

"Okay, I'll try not to mind if I do. I'll have fun."

But it didn't feel fun as she waited to go in. Aunt Olwen tied her number round her waist. She was seventeen.

"But I'm not seventeenth to go in," she complained.

"It doesn't seem to work like that," said Aunt Olwen. "You're seventeen now and for the rest of the day." Mory was horribly nervous. She peeped into the school in time to see the girl before her come down the centre line, halt and salute. White boards marked out the size of the dressage arena and the letter markers stood on stalk legs.

"Walk round to the judge," said Aunt Olwen, "and give her your number. She'll toot her horn when she's ready for you to begin. Good luck."

Mory urged Dancer forward. She went in warily. What were those white boards? They weren't there before, she seemed to say, side-stepping to get a good look.

"Don't be a daft pony," Mory whispered, although

she knew she was not supposed to speak. Two people were sitting in a silver four-wheel-drive vehicle at the far end of the school behind the letter C. One of them was the judge. Sitting as relaxed as she could with such a bad dose of nerves, Mory walked Dancer round the arena and waited by the car.

"And you are?" said a voice from within.

"Mory Harper, number seventeen."

"Thank you."

I wish I wasn't so nervous, she thought, walking on. At the corner she trotted to the far end of the school, halted and trotted again circling ready to come in at A. Dancer was settling now. She'd got used to the strange white marker boards. The horn sounded. This was the moment. Enter trotting at A, down the centre line, halt at X and salute. Mory remembered that bit and came to halt, took the reins in her left hand, dropped her right to her side and bowed her head. The salute over she took a deep breath. Now to start.

They trotted on down the centre line. *Which way do I go?* Panic. Mory's mind went blank. She looked at the car window for inspiration and a face looked straight back at her smiling encouragement. Go left, the smile seemed to say. Of course it's left, a little voice whispered somewhere in her head. And left she went and as she trotted between H and E her route unfolded before her. She trotted, she cantered, she walked the well-worn pattern of movements. It

wasn't until trotting down the centre line for her final
halt and salute that she realized she had done the
whole test without forgetting once.

"Congratulations," said Aunt Olwen.

"Well done, Mory," said Cara.

"I remembered it," said Mory, laughing with relief.
"I can hardly believe it." She fished in her jacket
pocket for some peppermints. Dancer deserved one;
she'd been really good.

Caroline was next. She rode past with a look of
intense concentration.

"Good luck," Mory said on impulse. Caroline's
expression gave no hint of having heard. They
watched her from the doorway. Doughnut's usual
flowing gait was stilted and jerky and towards the end
of the test the pony was throwing her head in the air.

"Caroline's tense," whispered Cara. "She's giving
Doughnut a horrible time."

"When's it your turn?" Mory asked, confused by
wanting to be better than Caroline and sorry for her
at the same time.

"Next but one. Then it's Josh."

"Good luck, I'll come back then."

Mory rode off to find out about the Handy Pony
class, keen to know what terrible obstacles faced
Dancer. The course was set up in the field next to the
jumping arena. At the entrance was a board telling
competitors what they had to do. The winner would be
the one who completed all the tasks in the fastest time.

"Mmm," mused Mory and followed the plan. First you had to pick up a giant panda and carry it across a giant black and white zebra crossing. "Heck!" Then you had to go down an alley made of car tyres, jump a ditch with blue polythene in the bottom – pretend water – and two poles over it. After that you had to go under an arch covered with bunting, dash in and out of eight bending poles, stop, dismount and pick an apple from a bucket of water with your teeth – no hands allowed! Remount the *wrong* side, take a flag from a striped cone, charge fifty yards to another cone, stick the flag in that and dash to the finish. "Help, help, help!" gasped Mory and burst out laughing. The girl beside her also looking laughed with her.

"The worst bit will be getting the apple," the girl said.

"Will it?" said Mory, wondering if she'd ever get round.

Watching the others doing their dressage tests soothed Mory's anxiety about the Handy Pony course. Cara rode really well and so did Josh. But if she had to choose between them Cara did the better test, her years of experience showed and Mory wondered if she might come first until she watched Lionel ride Elveston Tawney. The pony danced for Lionel, who rode a gentle, accurate, calm test. Could anyone ride better than that? thought Mory, bursting with admiration. Why wasn't his dad here to watch? Surely he would be proud.

"Well done," Mory said as he came out. The others echoed her.

"Thank you, Lionel," said Megan coming up to him and putting her hand on his arm. "That was a super test."

"Reckon they'll want him after that," he said. "He went well."

"I think they will," Megan replied.

"He's a good boy," said Lionel running his hand down the pony's sleek neck. Mory noticed the wistful way he said it. It was obvious there were people watching who wanted to buy Tawney. After a test like that Mory was sure he would be sold.

# FIFTEEN

## *Jump Off*

Mory wondered how Dancer would do as she watched Cara ride the Handy Pony course. Misty did it perfectly. Cara took ages getting the apple from the bucket but so had everyone else. Now it was Josh's turn. Rustler crossed the zebra crossing, trotted between the car tyres and leapt the ditch as if it was nothing. He whizzed under the bunting, spun through the bending poles and halted sharply on his haunches. Jumping off, Josh undid his hat and, hanging on to Rustler's reins, plunged his head into the apple bucket. Within seconds he emerged spluttering with an apple between his teeth. His hat back on he mounted easily from the wrong side, grabbed the flag and charged. He spun Rustler round the cone and with a deadly aim slotted the flag in before racing for the finish. The whole thing was breathtakingly fast.

That is going to take some beating, thought Mory. It was her turn. She passed Josh on his way out, grinning and patting Rustler. She trotted Dancer round in a large circle waiting for the bell to start. She feared disaster but told herself it didn't matter.

The bell rang and she crossed the starting line, trotting to the giant panda. To her utter amazement Dancer waited while she picked it up. At the giant zebra crossing there was a slight hesitation but Dancer trotted across allowing Mory to deposit the panda on its stand. Mory took the pony positively towards the alley of car tyres. Dancer snorted at them.

"Get on with you," said Mory sternly. Dancer backed away. Mory's heels drummed at her sides. Suddenly, she shot forward and dashed between the tyres as fast as she could go. Mory told her how wonderful she was and gathered her together for the ditch. Again she urged the pony forward, not letting up until they were in the air, then she pushed on towards the bunting. Dancer was going forward now and shot under it. Mory turned for the bending poles and they weaved between them.

"Good girl," said Mory, stopping by the apple bucket. Like Josh she took off her hat and plunged after an apple. Unlike Josh it took her two goes to get one. On with the hat she mounted from the wrong side. Thank goodness they'd practised. She urged Dancer towards the flag. Dancer skipped away sideways and they swung round three times before she let Mory pick it up. They cantered on steadily towards the last task, Mory taking careful aim. At the last moment Dancer shied at the bright orange cone and Mory had to swing round and come in again. But Dancer stood while she slotted the flag in and they were able to turn and canter for the finish.

"Well done, lovely pony," she said, patting the black neck. It was a million times better than she expected. She was pleased and relieved. Dancer was getting the idea. There was hope for them yet.

"Well done," said Cara.

"Great," said Josh. "You did everything. Some ponies have got eliminated."

"Much better than I could have dreamed. Patience wins out in the end."

"Guess who won the dressage?" said Cara.

"Lionel."

"Yup. Josh was fourth. I was third and guess where you were?"

"Tell me."

"Fifth!"

"Fifth," she repeated, her mouth dropping open. "Hell's bells, that's brilliant."

As the six winners cantered round the indoor school in a lap of honour, rosettes flying from their bridles, or in Mory's case from her teeth as remedy against Dancer spooking, Mory realized that Caroline hadn't been placed. Boy, would she be mad to be beaten by Dancer.

Mory didn't dwell on the thought being quickly distracted by David taking photographs and by

Sheila, Aunt Olwen and Uncle Glyn showering congratulations. There was still the show jumping and the flag race to go. It was bliss.

"And Josh has won the Handy Pony," said Aunt Olwen. "Cara was third. Well done both of you. Off you go. They're waiting to hand out the rosettes."

"Did you see Dancer go round?" said Mory as the others trotted off. "She did everything."

"We watched every nerve-racking moment," said Sheila laughing. "She was wonderful."

"Please will you look after my rosette?"

"Of course." The purple, mauve and white ribbons danced in the breeze. "What pretty colours. Perfect for a first rosette," said Sheila. Mory was in heaven.

The novice jumping started punctually at half past two. There were lots of competitors including Caroline and Josh. Lionel and Cara were in the next class, the intermediate with bigger jumps. So Lionel offered to walk the course with Mory to help her work out distances and strides. Cara went with Josh. The course had ten jumps that thrilled and alarmed.

"Don't panic," said Lionel as if guessing. "They're not big. The fallen oak is bigger than these. But it's more tricky, this. Jumps come fast. You got to think ahead."

They walked between the starting posts to the first jump, red and white cross poles with a pole across the top.

"Nice easy first jump," said Lionel. "Start steady. Once over you've got to turn a bit for the next to come at it straight." He pointed to a staircase of rustic poles. "Nice and inviting." He started to pace between the jumps. Mory did the same. "Eight strides?" Mory agreed. "You've got to keep turning to come round for this." He crossed to a fence filled with yellow and blue plastic drums with wide white wings. "Push on for this and then you got three strides to the parallel poles." Mory paced them out. "To make it three keep pushing on, then once over steady up as you keep on the turn. You've got to line up for the wall and make sure you go round with the inside leg leading." He grinned. "It's not that bad, is it?" Mory's face was a picture of misery.

"It's all right for you, you've done it before." Lionel laughed.

"You'll do it easy peasy," he said. "Just listen."

"I am," she said.

"Come at the wall straight and push on at it, keep your head up, look over it. Go for it. As you come over you need to change leading leg."

"How?"

"Don't worry about it. If she's wrong come down to a trot and ask for the right leg as you start to turn."

"Heck, Lionel." They walked to the next, a pyramid.

"More rustic poles," said Lionel. "Got a ground line." They paced between the pyramid and the upright poles that followed.

"Nine strides," they agreed.

"Two strides between the upright and the parallels. She'll be going well by this time. Over and turn. Same leading leg." The next jump was parallel rustic poles with fir tree filler. "Nice and solid," continued Lionel. "Then turn into the last, the zigzag planks. Don't be fooled by those planks. They knock off dead easy. Just 'cos it's last don't rush it." He grinned. "Got it?"

"I think so."

"She'll pop you round," he said. "But you've got to help her. Ponies like Rustler and Doughnut do it for you. Experienced, see. You've got to ride Dancer. You can. No problem." It was good to know that Lionel felt confident. Mory was far from feeling it. Back in the collecting ring Mory took Dancer's reins from Sheila. Lionel gave her a leg up and wished her luck.

"Don't rush," he said. "Give her time. Same in the jump off. You'll want to go fast but don't. Forget the clock."

"Who says I'll make the jump off," said Mory. Her nerves were making her feel queasy. Lionel didn't say anything else, just gave another annoying grin. Sheila patted her arm sympathetically.

"You enjoy it," she said. "Remember – partners! Just keep together and have fun." Mory nodded, patted Dancer's neck and went to warm up.

Mory queued to jump the practice jump behind

Caroline and Doughnut and when Caroline caught her eye Mory gave her an encouraging smile. It was cut dead. Mory shrugged, followed on behind and jumped the fence neatly. Dancer was eager and there was a hint of a buck. Mory didn't want to shatter that confidence. We go slowly, slowly, she thought.

Mory's name was fifth to go on the board which gave her and Dancer the opportunity to watch some of the other competitors go round. They stood at the edge of the collecting ring. A chestnut pony charged the course. It went clear until the last, when, just as Lionel said it would, with a tap, the top plank fell.

Josh was next. Mory wished him luck as he trotted past. He cantered Rustler neatly between the jumps until the bell rang. Mory's heart was in her mouth. She watched him jump the poles and the staircase and then could watch no more. She turned away. Two more riders to go and it would be her.

"A clear round for number twenty-two, Josh Harper on Rustler. The next to go is number twenty-five, Caroline Spencer on Doughnut." She decided to watch Caroline and turned back. Doughnut was a confident little pony, but was having to battle with a rider who was less than so. Yet round they went. The stiffer Caroline got the more nearly unseated she became. She almost came off after the wall. After that she seemed to relax a little as if that was the worst she could do and now it could only get better. Round they came to jump the rustic poles with the fir tree filler.

They were wrong and Doughnut, quick as a flash, put in an extra stride and cleared it. Caroline ended half way up her neck. On to the last which they also cleared. Lionel was right. Doughnut knew exactly what she was doing.

"We're going to try and be a bit neater than that," whispered Mory. "We'll go nice and steady and keep a wonderful rhythm." Mory didn't watch any more. She trotted Dancer round and popped her over the practice fence for the last time. When her name was called she felt ready. This was the moment.

"Come on girl, off we go!"

They trotted into the ring followed by a chorus of good luck calls.

"We need good luck and some good judgement," she said, running a hand down Dancer's neck. "Let's hope we've got both." She cantered in a circle between the jumps, looking and remembering as she went. She knew the way, it was indelibly marked on her memory. Now it only needed the bell. Canter, canter, canter, it rang. They were between the starting posts. Dancer's ears pricked.

"Steady," said Mory sitting up. The cross poles came towards them and they were in the air already, turning for the staircase. One, two, three and they were over, turn, turn, turn and ahead the yellow and blue drums. Mory checked, saw the stride and pushed on. They landed and stride, stride, stride, jump. Dancer was enjoying this. She got a bit strong.

"Steady," said Mory sitting up and giving a pull. "Steady." The pony came back to her and they turned for the wall. Mory saw the stride, she felt Dancer hesitate for a moment. Mory urged her forward and there was a release of energy as Dancer decided to go. Whatever the wall was to Dancer she didn't like it and the jump was huge, but Mory was ready for it.

"Good girl," she said. "Good girl." She looked down briefly. Wrong leg. She slowed to a trot, turned and cantered again. They were right now and the pyramid was upon them. They jumped it and Mory was counting nine in to the upright poles. Jump stride, stride jump, out over the parallel and turn to the next, the parallel with the fir tree filler. Dancer had a lovely rhythm now. She jumped this in her stride and turned for the final fence. The zigzag stripes on the planks flashed garish orange. Dancer's ears pricked and Mory knew she was going to refuse.

"Go on," she commanded. Her voice stern, her eyes on the finish. "Go on." Dancer surged forward as if from a starting gate and jumped the orange monster with a huge jump. There was applause from the spectators as Mory burst across the finish. She flung her arms round the pony's neck, patting and hugging her as she cantered on round the arena. They had done it. They had gone clear. What more in the world was there to wish for?

"And number seventeen goes clear. Mory Harper on her own Midnight Dancer. The next to jump is

Sharon Lock on Mr Blue, number thirty-one."

Back in the collecting ring Mory jumped off and fished in her pocket for the peppermints.

"You really deserve them," she said giving Dancer three. "Good girl." Dancer chewed with relish, dropping slobber all over Mory's arm. "Thank you very much," said Mory laughing. "This is my new jacket. Have some respect." Then she realized Lionel had got it right. They'd gone clear which meant they'd have to jump again in the jump off.

Altogether there were five clear rounds and Mory was drawn last but one to go in the jump off. It was daunting having to go round again.

"It's not all of it," said Lionel. "Fences three, four and nine are out. The fences left are a bit bigger but nothing like the height Dancer's already jumped. Like I said, don't think about the clock. Take it steady."

This time Mory did watch Josh go round. He set off as if he meant business. He was slick and fast and Rustler gave his all. But Josh cut the corner into the wall just that bit too much and had a brick out. He was extremely disappointed. Caroline was next. She seemed to trust Doughnut more this time but she too came unstuck by a sharp turn to the wall and Doughnut stopped. Caroline was furious. Mory watched aghast as Caroline raised her whip but before she could strike it flew from her hand as if some unseen force had grabbed it. Mory was outraged. It was obvious Doughnut couldn't have jumped from that crazy angle. Apart from the refusal Caroline went clear. Thanks to Doughnut, Mory thought.

Turning Dancer back to the practice jump Mory popped her over it once just to remind her. They were the next but one to go.

"We're going to do it the same as before," she told Dancer. "Only this time there're not so many jumps." They stood ready to go and watched Sarah, their friend from school, whizz round on her pony Magpie. She too came unstuck at the wall, and like Josh, took a brick out but otherwise went clear.

"Four faults for Magpie in a time of forty-four seconds," said the announcer. "And the last but one to go, Mory Harper on Midnight Dancer." Into the ring they went. Mory cantered a large circle, casting her eye over the new route. She had no intention of racing to beat the clock. Her sole intent was to get Dancer safely round for a second time. The bell rang.

Mory sensed a different Dancer. The pony set off purposefully, ears pricked. *I know what this is all about*, she seemed to be saying. They were over the cross poles and the staircase before Mory had time to think and then they turned, looping wide unlike the others, to come in straight at the imposing wall. This time there was no hesitation. Mory prepared herself for a gigantic leap but they came at it just right and the jump was perfect. They picked up their rhythm and turned in the other direction, this time with the correct leading leg. Dancer jumped the pyramid and Mory counted out nine rhythmic paces and pushed on over the upright and one, two three, up and over the parallel. Just the planks left. They cantered steadily to them in a gentle curve. Dancer's ear pricked forward. *I know about these* she seemed to say and without the slightest hesitation sprang into the air and a moment later cantered between the finishing posts. It was another clear round.

Mory grinned from ear to ear. What a pony! What a brilliant pony!

Mory dismounted and got out the peppermints which Dancer nudged for. "If Sharon Lock goes clear," said Lionel joining her, "it puts you second. If she doesn't …" He raised an eyebrow. Just then Mory didn't care where she came and idly watched the slick pair in the ring jump a fast clear round. But at the last Mr Blue took off too far back. He tried hard but just tipped the top plank with a hind leg. It wobbled and slowly fell.

"You've won!" shouted Lionel, patting Mory on the back. Dancer jumped back startled. "You've won!"

"I don't believe it," Mory said.

"I knew you would."

"An unbelievable fluke," said Caroline standing nearby. She turned away with a sour look. Lionel and Mory hardly heard they were laughing so much and

Lionel patted Mory on the back and Mory patted Dancer and gave her more peppermints. Then they both spat and palm to palm shook a jubilant handshake. Dancer had done it and had proved what Mory knew all along, that she was fantastic!

# Epilogue

The day of the Penyworlod Show had been quite beyond Mory's best imaginings. She lifted her paintbrush glistening with black paint and let it slide across whiteness. Dancer! To be immortalized on the pottery wall. As the brush formed the shape of her pony Mory remembered everything about the show. The dressage test, the Handy Pony competition, the crazy flag race where once she got the idea Dancer had raced her best along with Misty and Rustler. True, Tawney had pranced about a bit, but still they had come third. But best and most exciting of all – the show jumping. The glory of that red rosette with the gold 1st. Dancer had proved herself and so had she. Mum was right, this was only the beginning. There was the summer to come with more shows, more jumping and riding, riding, riding out across the hills.

"Yesterday," Mory announced to the Dancer on the wall, "was the best day of my life." She stood back to admire her work, then added, "So far!" And a smile of anticipation lit up her face.

# The Babysitters Club

Need a babysitter? Then call the Babysitters Club. Kristy Thomas and her friends are all experienced sitters. They can tackle any job from rampaging toddlers to a pandemonium of pets. To find out all about them, read on!

*Our favourite Babysitters are detectives too! Don't miss the new series of Babysitters Club Mysteries:*

*Available now:*

### No 1: Stacey and the Missing Ring
When Stacey's accused of stealing a valuable ring from a new family she's been sitting for, she's devastated – Stacey is *not* a thief!

### No 2: Beware, Dawn!
Just *who* is the mysterious "Mr X" who's been sending threatening notes to Dawn and phoning her while she's babysitting, *alone*?

### No 3: Mallory and the Ghost Cat
Mallory thinks she's solved the mystery of the spooky cat cries coming from the Craine's attic. But Mallory can *still* hear crying. Will Mallory find the *real* ghost of a cat this time?

### No 4: Kristy and the Missing Child
When little Jake Kuhn goes missing, Kristy can't stop thinking about it. Kristy makes up her mind. She *must* find Jake Kuhn . . . wherever he is!

### No 5: Mary Anne and the Secret in the Attic
Mary Anne is curious about her mother, who died when she was just a baby. Whilst rooting around in her creepy old attic Mary Anne comes across a secret she never knew . . .

### No 6: The Mystery at Claudia's House
Just what is going on? Who has been ransacking Claudia's room and borrowing her make-up and clothes? Something strange is happening at Claudia's house and the Babysitters are determined to solve the mystery . . .

# Hippo Fantasy

Lose yourself in a whole new world, a world where anything is possible – from wizards and dragons, to time travel and new civilizations ... Gripping, thrilling, scary and funny by turns, these Hippo Fantasy titles will hold you captivated to the very last page.

## *The Night of Wishes*
Michael Ende (author of *The Neverending Story*)

It's New Year's Eve, and Beelzebub Preposteror, sorceror and evil-doer, has only seven hours to complete his annual share of villainous deeds and *completely destroy the world!*

## *Rowan of Rin*
Emily Rodda

The witch Sheba has made a mysterious prophecy, which is like a riddle. A riddle Rowan must solve if he is to find out the secret of the mountain and save Rin from disaster ...

## *The Wednesday Wizard*
Sherryl Jordan

Denzil, humble apprentice to the wizard Valvasor, is in a real pickle. When he tries to reach his master to warn him of a dragon attack, he mucks up the spell and ends up seven centuries into the future!

## *The Practical Princess*
Jay Williams

The Practical Princess has the gift of common sense. And when you spend your days tackling dragons and avoiding marriage to unsuitable suitors, common sense definitely comes in useful!